MELT
MY
HEART

*Other books by Bethany Rutter*

No Big Deal

# MELT MY HEART

### BETHANY RUTTER

MACMILLAN CHILDREN'S BOOKS

First published 2020 by Macmillan Children's Books
an imprint of Pan Macmillan
20 New Wharf Road, London N1 9RR
Associated companies throughout the world
www.panmacmillan.com

ISBN 978-1-5290-4116-3

1 3 5 7 9 8 6 4 2

A CIP catalogue record for this book is available from
the British Library.

Printed and bound by CPI Group (UK) Ltd, Croydon CR0 4YY

*For Charlie*

# CHAPTER ONE

*New things! New things! New things!* I chant in my head as my feet pound the pavement. I have no idea how Daisy does this. My chest hurts. My calves hurt. Even my actual bum hurts. I try to distract myself by taking in my surroundings but without making eye contact with passers-by. My lungs are burning and there's that metallic taste in my mouth. I definitely don't feel stress free and relaxed. Please, where are those endorphins I hear so much about? But it's a new thing so it must be good, right?!

I let myself slow down to a jog as a flock of seagulls wheel overhead, squawking raucously, swooping towards the ground, scouting for a few discarded chips. The picturesque seaside scene is usually enough to distract me from anything, but today my anxiety is sitting on my chest like a lead weight.

*Go running*, they said. *It'll be fun*, they said. Famous last words.

'If you're feeling stressed you should go to the gym or something,' Daisy had said to me only yesterday. That's the kind of thing Daisy says semi-regularly. 'I'm thinking of taking up wrestling at uni to battle the first-year stress.'

'What are you on about?' I'd asked her, incredulous, before realizing that Daisy's zeal for trying new things is less weird than my tendency to stay firmly within my comfort zone.

It's the first week of July and I can already feel the summer slipping away from me. So I'm trying to prepare myself for the fact that at the end of the summer I'm going to university hundreds of miles away, and I'll be meeting so many new people and doing so many new things. I'm not ready. Not yet. But maybe I can become ready. I can start challenging myself to shake up my life a bit before I get there. Say yes to things. Try stuff I've never tried before. I have no doubt it'll be good for me. Even if sometimes it makes my bum hurt. A summer of new things, if you will.

*Bloody hell.* I dare to take a look at the timer on my phone and immediately want to dropkick it off the end of the pier when I discover I've been running for a mere two and a half minutes. The honk of a horn from a passing car pulls me out of my anger. I can't tell what they're saying because I've got my headphones in but I *can* tell a group of lads is leaning out the window and yelling at me. Fat girl jogging. It must have simply been *too* hard for them to resist. Heaven forbid that a non-skinny, non-athletic girl could want to go for a run in peace (or whatever kind of peace this new sweaty hell is).

I suppress an eye roll and look away and try to focus on running running running, but as soon as I do, I feel something make brief but solid contact with my shoulder and bounce off it. Clattering to the ground in front of me is a can. A literal can. It's not even empty: it rolls around at my feet, spraying its sticky, brightly coloured contents over the pavement but mercifully *not* on my trainers. I look up, my general anxiety transformed into specific fury, and yet I'm unsurprised. It doesn't matter what I think about my body, how generally at peace I am with it, I still have to put up with this ludicrous behaviour from the outside world.

That's it. If I was looking for a sign that I should give up, here it is. I tried running, I didn't like it, and the universe didn't like it either. So I accept that I have ground to a halt and instantly feel better, the air returning to my lungs. My name is Lily Rose and I don't really know who I am, but I know I'm not a runner.

And anyway, there are other, less humiliating ways to push me out of my comfort zone. I'm sure of it. But maybe I need someone to keep me accountable so I don't just give up on *all* of them the way I've given up on this . . .

I head back along the pavement that runs by the side of the pebbly beach. It doesn't take long for my breath to return to me, but I'm still sweating by the time I turn off the road that follows the coast and get to the petrol station by our house. What can I say, I'm a sweater! I come from a family of sweaters, plus I've got what someone might euphemistically call 'extra insulation', so there was really no hope for me. I push open the door of the shop, eager to get myself a hard-earned gleaming tinny of cherry Coke to quench my thirst, swipe one from the fridge and head up to the counter to pay.

The dude behind the till raises his eyes from his phone and realizes it's one of his regular customers. They change the staff here pretty often but he's been around for a few months now, and he's friendly whenever I come in. His badge tells me his name's Jay. 'Hey!' he says. 'All alone today?'

'Yeah.' I smile, fishing in the tiny zip pocket at the back of my leggings for some change.

'Where's your friend?'

'Which friend?' I ask, even though I automatically assume he means Cassie, since she's essentially the only person I know who could be described as a friend. Also, she's pretty memorable.

'You know who I mean! The girl you're always with! The pretty one! She's got that same long, dark hair as you,' Jay says, gesticulating in exasperation as if I'm being deliberately stupid.

Ah. There it is.

'My sister?' I reply, raising my eyebrows and setting the coins down on the counter.

'No, not your sister,' he replies instinctively. 'She couldn't be your . . .' Jay trails off, realizing he's very much put his foot in it.

'Twin sister, actually. Thanks!' I shrug it off breezily even though, frankly, I hate it when this happens. I put time and energy into not comparing myself to her, into honouring our same-but-different-ness, but there's always that little niggling reminder that Daisy is the desirable twin and I am . . . well, just me. I accept my change and zip it back into my pocket. As I trudge out of the petrol station, I crack open my icy-cold cherry Coke and let it hit my tongue. It's exactly what I need to take the heat off this embarrassing exchange. I peek back and see Jay standing behind the counter looking perplexed and slightly awkward. Poor dude.

The thing is, guys would never shout at my sister from a passing car. Actually, that's not true: they really would, except they would be yelling something more . . . sexually suggestive, and it wouldn't be accompanied by a projectile. It's not Jay's fault for not realizing we're related, let alone twin sisters. The truth is, we're identical in every way . . . except she's thin and I'm fat. That's it. We both have long, dark, straight hair that we wear with a middle parting.

Dark, heavy eyebrows. Light skin. Freckles on our faces and arms. Eyes so bright green that they almost look fake. But that difference in body shape, or rather body *size*, is enough to have people scratching their heads.

I sip my drink as I walk back round the corner to our little house and let myself in. Our candy-pink cottage covered in creeping ivy is more picture-book cute than the rest of the conservatively coloured houses on our street. When Crystal, our fluffy white cat (and the latest addition to the Rose family), is sitting in the window, it looks even more adorable. Like it's a serene seaside residence for discerning ladies.

'Hello, baby,' Mum yells from the living room. 'Where have you been?'

I slouch in, nonchalantly. 'Nowhere.'

'Have you been . . .' She squints at me, surveying my trainers and my probably still-pink face. 'Running?'

I sit on the sofa with a sigh and wriggle my feet out of my trainers. Deflection seems like the best option here. 'I have no idea what would give you that impression.'

'Because you know you're perfect as you are, right?' Mum says. It's sweet that she thinks this. I know not all mums are quite so chill.

'Mum – let's be real here. I'm not running because I've suddenly decided I need to be a size eight. Just felt like trying out something new.'

'Oh . . .' She frowns. 'Why wouldn't you go with Daisy, then? She's always out running.'

'Exactly,' I say, a bit sullenly.

'Oh . . .' she says again. A good thing about our mum is that she knows not to probe too far into the mysterious ways of the sisters.

She doesn't need to know how quickly Daisy would get frustrated with how slowly I run, or how I gave up after a couple of minutes. She absolutely doesn't need to know that while Daisy has always been like a machine that won't quit, I've been struggling to keep up. But I guess if I had gone with her, I wouldn't have been pelted with a can of Red Bull. You win some, you lose some.

'Where is she, anyway?' I ask.

'Where do you think she is?'

I head through the kitchen where the smell of Mum's cooking is perfuming the air wonderfully, push the back door open and lean against the white-painted frame to observe my sister at work in the garden, crouched down on the ground with her headphones in. As if she can sense that I'm there, she raises her head, the change in position making the sun glint off her identically shiny hair.

My sister's outdoor pursuits are a mystery to me. I like to watch her work, just to see what she's up to. I can ask her what she's been planting or what she's been using to make things grow, but I don't really understand it. The only part I do understand is the quiet dedication I see when she's out here in the little square garden — or as our mum calls it: Daisy's domain. The garden is to her what a canvas is to me: pure potential. The start of something beautiful.

'Lil, are you spying on me?' Daisy asks with a smile as she pulls her headphones out. She's the only person who calls me Lil. I don't really like it but I can tolerate it from my twin sister.

'Maybe a bit,' I say, snaking my arm back into the kitchen and dunking the empty Coke can into the recycling bin without looking. 'What you got there?'

'Check this out!' she says, gleefully revealing a small pile of slim carrots. 'They're going to be so sweet and delicious even on their own, I just know it.'

'I'm excited to reap the rewards of your hard work.'

'Oh, it wasn't that hard.' She smiles modestly.

'I'm excited to reap the rewards of your easy work.'

Daisy laughs, wiping some sweat from her brow and leaving a brown streak of soil in its place. That's the other reason guys like her — she's the perfect girl next door. She knows she's pretty and doesn't care. She's at ease in the world. She's not a tangle of stress and fear like me. Maybe she would have been a good influence on me if we'd stuck to our original plan, and decided to go to uni together. As it is, I don't know how many more delicious Daisy-grown carrots I'll get to eat come September. 'Hey, make sure Crystal doesn't get out.'

'Oh, shit, you're right. I keep forgetting about that.' Crystal has to be kept indoors for reasons we're not entirely clear on but accept none the less because Mum knows best.

Daisy stands and brushes the soil off herself, gathers her carrots from the ground and surveys me. 'How come you're wearing workout gear?'

I gasp in mock offence. 'As if I never work out!'

She rolls her eyes. 'You don't.'

'Just trying out the ol' athleisure trend,' I lie. I used to tell Daisy everything – there was a time when we were inseparable. But things change, I guess . . . we changed. Or the ways we were always different became more pronounced. Anyway, now that I've got Cassie, who just takes me as I am, no judgement, I don't really have the energy to take on any more of Daisy's assumptions. So I decide not to tell her about my three-minute 'run'. She'd probably read something into it, like I'm going on a mad pre-uni transformation to get skinny over the summer so I can rock up at Leeds as a whole new Lily. At some point, she'll finally get that I like my body the way it is, and maybe then things will go back to the way they used to be. But I'm not going to hold my breath.

Daisy dumps the carrots in a colander in the sink and heads upstairs to shower while I set the table for dinner, which turns out to be Thai.

'How was work?' I ask my mum once we've sat down, blowing on my spoonful of tom yum soup, which, as with everything my mum serves, is absolutely boiling.

'Oh, fine, nothing much to report,' she says before gulping down a huge mouthful with no regard for the inside of her mouth.

'Did you have to . . .' Daisy raises her eyes from her bowl. 'You know . . .' She grimaces and mimes injecting the air with a syringe.

'No, not today, thank god.'

'Phew!' Daisy and I say in unison. We know our mum would never volunteer information about having to put a pet down because it makes us too sad and yet we can't help but ask about it, like morbid little ghouls.

'But!' Mum says, raising a finger to silence us. 'Tom Greenwell and his dad were in with their cat today.' She sips her soup. 'He was asking about you.'

'What a clever cat,' I say.

I don't even need to look up to know Mum's comment was directed at Daisy, not me. I shift in my chair, grudgingly reminded of one of many times Daisy liked the same guy as me.

I always had a little bit of a crush on Tom, but last summer I'd made the mistake of whispering it to Daisy, my tongue blue from the Slush Puppie inching its way up the straw as we walked home from the beach. She said that she liked him too, and announced that she was going to ask him out. She never did, of course – it's not really her style to be the 'asker' rather than the 'asked' – but she had marked her territory, which was enough to put me off. Tom was in *her* league. And I was very much in mine.

'What was he saying?' Daisy asks, eagerly. To be fair, Tom Greenwell is very cute. What can I say, I have good taste.

'Oh, nothing much,' Mum says. 'Just wanted to know what you were up to this summer. I told him he could find you at the garden centre if he was particularly desperate.' This makes Daisy squeal a little bit before grimacing.

'But my work uniform is so *ugly*,' she moans.

'Yeah, but you're not,' I say with a shrug. 'I'm sure Tom can see past a sick-green shirt and weird pinstripe trousers to your true beauty.'

'The garden centre uniform is not *that* bad,' says Mum. 'My school uniform was—'

'Yes, Mum, we know!' Daisy and I groan in unison.

'Brown wool blazer, fawn wool jumper, beige shirt, green tie, dark brown pleated skirt and brown tights,' I continue, holding up a finger for each item.

'Oh and flat, brown lace-up shoes,' Daisy finishes for me.

'It was awful!' says Mum. 'No chance of meeting boys in *that*. That's how they wanted it. Anyway, what about the boy at the cinema you said you liked? I feel like we've been hearing about him for months.'

Daisy furrows her brow. 'I don't know, I haven't been in a while what with exams and stuff. I should see if he's still there. He's even cuter than Tom. Nice blue eyes. Cool accent.' She has a determined look in her eye, like it's never occurred to her that anything might stand in her way. Assured.

'I can't even think of the last time I went to the cinema,' says Mum.

'Me neither . . . maybe I'll see if Cassie wants to go after work one day,' I say.

'*Work*,' says Mum, raising her eyebrows. 'It's funny hearing you two say that. You're just tiny babies to me.'

'Yeah, if I have to work it might as well be scooping ice cream with my best friend.' My phone vibrates. 'Speak of the devil.'

It is Cassie, even if it doesn't say it's Cassie – I saved her in my phone as 'Ice Queen' to reflect her status as heiress to Weston Bay and Seaforth's premier ice-cream business.

It works even better because she's the least frosty person I know.

I have two words for you

Which are?

Chocolate orange

That's gonna be a HIT

My dad's been working on it for ages trying to get it just right. Make sure your scoopin' arm is feeling STRONG tomorrow

My SPIRIT is going to be feeling strong tomorrow. I am sincerely so hyped I get to spend the summer with you even if we're working

It doesn't feel like work when you're there tbh

We've been working on the ice-cream stand for a few days now and, I've got to say, she's not wrong. We've hit our stride. The days pass pretty quickly. *And* we're getting paid for it.

Idk if I'm actually fun enough for that to be true 🙍

DO YOU UNDERSTAND THERE IS LITERALLY NO ONE I WOULD RATHER TOIL WITH THAN YOU????

I grin and turn my phone face-down on the table.

'Little custard tart things for afters?' Mum asks.

'Always,' I say. A firm favourite of ours since we were little. Daisy used to eat the tart then bite on the silver cases they came in, leaving tiny toothmarks in the mangled foil.

'Not for me,' says Daisy. 'I'm being good.' I roll my eyes.

'It's your choice but I think you're being ridiculous,' says Mum.

Daisy sighs, disgruntled. 'I just want to look optimally hot when I get to uni, is that a crime?'

'Your optimal hotness is whatever you look like right now. I promise.' Mum is good at reassuring Daisy. Better than I would be, anyway. To be honest, she's good at reassuring both of us.

I don't say anything. I don't think Daisy has figured out how these comments affect me. At least, I hope she hasn't. It'd be worse if she was saying them knowingly.

'We'll wash up,' I say once the tarts have been reduced to shortbread crumbs on the plate, volunteering on behalf of Daisy.

'Good girls,' Mum says, winking at us. 'Well, since you're taking care of this, I'm going to watch back-to-back episodes of *Four in a Bed* if you would care to join me when your domestic labour is done.'

Daisy and I turn the radio on and dance to cheesy music while she washes and I dry, careful not to drop bowls in a fit of Phil Collins-induced mania.

Our mum's voice cuts through from the living room into the intro of another eighties masterpiece. 'Lily!'

'Yes?' I call back, turning the radio down.

'I forgot to tell you – there's a letter for you from Leeds.'

It feels like a fist has tightened around my heart.

'Oh, OK . . .' I say, hopefully loud enough for her to hear. 'I'll open it when I'm done in here.' Daisy inhales sharply and twitches her nose, her universal symbol of disapproval. I guess she's a bit annoyed about us not going to uni together anymore. She doesn't notice my shaking hands. I was meant to be going to Bristol, same as Daisy. That's what we had talked about. But when the offers came through and Daisy accepted hers straight away, I felt like maybe it was time for me to separate from her a bit. Go my own way. That's the plan I deviated from. Now, of course, I don't know what I was thinking. What I *do* know is I feel like I'm thinking about it all the time.

When I start feeling like this, I don't feel like I can make my body do *anything*. It's like a tightly wound spring: all tension. I barely hold it together while we finish the washing-up and then I slip upstairs, swiping the letter from the little table in the hall.

Daisy's world may be the garden but my sanctuary is upstairs, in my room at the back of the house. Our small bedrooms are crowded together up here: Mum's is painted a soothing mint green, Daisy's a sugary lilac, and then . . . there's the quiet chaos of mine.

It's not just the *stuff* – books stacked everywhere, art supplies overflowing from every surface, canvases leaning against the walls and the cupboards – it's the walls. I'm not saying my mum was wrong to let me have free rein on my bedroom, but if she ever wants to sell the cottage my bedroom is going to need a complete makeover.

The two walls that make up the corner of the room by the door are painted a flat, neutral white, with my bed pushed against the side that shares a wall with Daisy's room. But the other two are a riot of colour and pattern and nature and leaves and vines and flowers in lush greens and vibrant blues and juicy pinks, like you're deep in the jungle on another planet. I suppose letting me do what I want with my room is like letting Daisy do what she wants with the garden. 'It's your home, too,' Mum always says.

As usual, just being in my space takes a little of the tension away. I can breathe here. But the letter in my hand is weighing me down. More than anything, I do not want to go to university in September. I do not want to leave my home. I do not want to leave my family. I do not want to leave comfort and familiarity. I absolutely, one hundred per cent, do not want to leave Cassie. But it's too late.

I flop down on my bed, my heart pounding against my ribcage. I take a deep breath and slide my thumb into the envelope, tearing it open in jagged waves. When I wriggle the letter free, all the words jumble together in a nauseating haze until I finally unscramble them. An accommodation letter. *What kind of halls do you want to be in? Catered or non-catered? How many people to a bathroom? How far from the campus? Do you mind sharing a room if push comes to shove?*

I let out a groan, close my eyes and take another deep breath. At this point I've had to accept that the whole university thing – the whole future thing – is hanging over me like a black cloud, and most of the time I can keep a lid on it. But every so often it becomes uncontainable and I have to confront the fact that at the end of this summer I'll have to leave my home.

It's such a dark thought that I haven't shared it with anyone, but I'm clinging on to the possibility that I might not get the results I need, and then I won't have to go away. Results day is in forty-one days – I counted them on the calendar. That's when it's real.

Until then, I'm going to enjoy myself. I've only got one summer left. The last summer.

One summer to get my head around all the ways my life is going to change.

# CHAPTER TWO

Another day, another dollar.

As I speed-walk from my house to the ice-cream stand on the green with its uninterrupted view of the sea, I know I'm running late. Not because I'm checking the time like a maniac, but because I pass the same people every day. I don't need a watch to tell me I'm *definitely* late. It was the same when I went to school. If the dad in the baseball hat with the big beard and the little girl with a pink scooter were already round the corner, I was probably going to miss the bus. If they hadn't made it round the corner yet, I still stood a chance. It's the summer holidays now, so no one's on the school run, but I've already missed the old man walking his Yorkshire Terrier. It's not quite the kind of small town where everyone knows everyone, but it just works. Predictably, comfortingly, a well-oiled machine. Like a toy town. *Late*. Definitely late.

Finally the pink-and-burgundy-striped ice-cream stand appears in the distance and I breathe a sigh of relief that Cassie is already there. It's still exciting that I get to spend the day with my favourite person. It's not as if it's particularly glamorous work, and we've only been doing it for a week, since her parents opened the cafe in Seaforth and needed two sensible young people to keep everything going here. But it's fun to be outside all day, seeing what the town is up to, and being able to chat to Cassie like we're still in the common room at college.

'What an amazing dress!' I call out to Cassie as I approach the stand. She looks up from the till, grins and gives me a twirl. Her midi smock dress is made of the most outrageous multicolour gingham and looks extremely cool with her chunky white trainers. Definitely a Cassie Palmer original.

Cassie likes making her own clothes not just because she can, but also because she's really tall. And kind of . . . big. Our bodies aren't the same – mine is softer, rounder, more conspicuously *there*. But there's something about her body – the scale of it and its presence – that makes me feel at home when I'm with her. I don't feel self-conscious with Cassie, or like she's judging me. She's too interesting to think that whether someone is fat or thin is a good basis on which to judge them.

'Why thank you.' She beams. 'Only yesterday this very dress was . . .' Cassie lowers her sunglasses in an invitation for me to guess.

'No offence but . . . a duvet cover?'

'Close! But nope!'

'Curtains? A tablecloth?'

'A tablecloth!'

'Amazing. Truly amazing.'

'I told you, I'll teach you how to use a sewing machine one day. If I can do it, anyone can.' I stop myself from telling her that's not strictly true. Cassie is very smart, but because she's mostly good at practical things like sewing and cooking she thinks that makes her less 'actually smart' than other people.

'Does it feel like . . .' Cassie says, squinting judiciously out towards the seafront while she yanks the lids off the ice cream tubs. 'There are more people here this year?'

'Yeah, I think you're right. Obviously it helps that the weather is incredible.'

'And it's Friday. Nice little long weekend from London.' She rummages in the cupboard underneath the counter and produces our matching baseball caps and aprons, which are surprisingly not too bad, just the iconic pink and burgundy stripe of all Palmer's Ices promotional materials. I tend to wear black to work to account for these colourful flourishes, but Cassie just lets the patterns and colours clash gloriously together.

'And it is indeed Friday!' I clap. It's the first weekend since we started working. Not that we've been working *too* hard.

'It's already twenty degrees at eleven o'clock in the morning on Friday the nineteenth of July. What a time to be alive,' she says, spreading her arms wide and tilting her face towards the sky. It's only going to get hotter from here. I dread to think what four o'clock will feel like.

'Global warming though, isn't it,' I say with a grimace, giving in to my inability to chill the hell out. If university doesn't kill me, maybe the heat death of the planet will.

'Live in the moment, my dude,' she says as the generator buzzes into action, ensuring our stock will stay nice and frozen. 'I think we're going to do a roaring trade today.'

I realize I'm beating my fingers against the palm of my hand in time to what Cassie's saying. It's something I've found myself doing lately when I feel overwhelmed by my thoughts. A way to find order in the chaos. 'Live in the moment' is the perfect phrase because it's five syllables, which means one for each finger before ending on the thumb. Ending on the thumb. Another perfect phrase. I tap it out a few times before realizing I should stop. I snap out of it, shaking my hand to loosen the fingers that were balled up in a fist. 'And if we do well here, imagine how business is gonna be in Seaforth — your parents opened the shop at exactly the right time.'

'Right?' Cassie gesticulates in exasperation. 'They were so cautious about opening a proper sit-in cafe but I knew it was a good idea. Plus, this way we get to hold the fort here without them breathing down our necks.'

I pause for a moment, checking there's enough change in the till (there is – the Palmers would never let something so important be overlooked). 'Some guys threw a can of Red Bull at me from a moving car last night.'

'What the hell?'

'Yeah . . . that's weird, right?'

'I mean . . . who does that?' Cassie asks, arching an eyebrow. 'It's madness! Did their parents not raise them right?' She looks genuinely furious on my behalf.

'Evidently not . . .' I say, glowing with delight at her indignation. 'I was running at the time.'

'Running?!'

'Don't sound so surprised!'

'No, no, I'm not! It's just very . . . plot twist-y.'

I sigh, remembering my burning thighs. 'It's not for me. And not just because of the projectile.' But as I say that I wonder if it's true. I'm already wondering, if I went out again, how much further I could go, even if I only lasted another thirty seconds or a minute.

Cassie shrugs. 'It's cool that you tried though. I like this spirit of adventure for you.'

Perfect. Cassie is the *perfect* person to get involved with my little scheme to try new things this summer. She'll be able to make all the terrifying stuff I'll be doing heaps of fun, and I'm never more comfortable or more myself than I am when I'm with her. 'Yeah, about that . . .'

'Oooh!' She looks enthused already.

'So. The inescapable truth is that, yes, I'm going to uni at the end of the summer.'

'Ah yes, that famous death sentence: university,' Cassie says drily.

'Look, you know I'm a little . . . wobbly about the whole thing. So to make everything slightly less wobbly, I want to hype myself up for The Big Change by trying something new every day, at least until I get my results.'

'I'm listening.' She nods, clearly intrigued now.

'And I would like to enlist your help. You know, to keep me accountable and motivated and tell me what to do when my imagination fails me. All the things you're good at.'

She beams. 'I am *honoured* you would think of me for this task. You got today's thing already?'

'Nope!'

'I'll figure something out,' she says, gazing mischievously out to sea, her big brown eyes focused on the still water.

We usually tag-team our brief lunch breaks and split whatever Cassie has brought with her: today's lunchtime special is orzotto with peas. She always brings enough for both of us, but just puts it all in one Tupperware box because we'll never be eating at the same time.

'Are you *sure* we can't eat lunch together?' I ask, digging in.

'If my mum drove past and saw the stand so much as *looking* like it was unattended, we would be unemployed so fast your head would spin.'

'So . . . that's a no, then?'

'That's a no.'

I suppose I should get used to not having someone to eat lunch with. Who knows who I'll be sitting with when I get to uni.

By the afternoon, our biceps are aching from all the scooping. Chocolate orange was, as predicted, a great success. By three o'clock we have to ring Cassie's mum at the cafe in Seaforth to tell her we're out of strawberry, and within half an hour she's run round another tub in their pink Palmer's Ices van. She barely parks, pulling up by the green and waving at Cassie to come over, then speeds off back to work, blowing kisses at us out of the window.

Cassie's mum, Tracy, is basically a business genius. She stepped in when Cassie was a baby and kind of took over the management of the whole company from Cassie's dad, who's a nice guy but has the complacency of someone running a family business whose success they take for granted. Since then, Tracy's expanded the brand from back in the day, when you could only really buy the ice cream from the creamery where it's made, to today, when it's distributed to the cutest cafes on this stretch of the coast, *and* has two sites of its own. She could give any president or tech founder a run for their money. Hey, if Facebook was run by a forty-three-year-old Jamaican woman maybe the world wouldn't be such a shitty place. Tracy Palmer's firm but fair command could take on Zuckerberg any day of the week.

'Still not tempted to take over the family business?' I ask Cassie.

'They wish,' she says, ruefully. Cassie's plans rather diverge from those of her parents. 'Look, at least an art foundation course gives me plausible deniability. As far as they know, I could be planning on doing Palmer's stuff after that.'

I look at her out of the corner of my eye. 'But you're not, right?'

'Nah. You and I both know I was put on this earth to stress out my mum.'

We stand in silence for a moment, contemplating our very separate futures. Only a few months ago my big bold decision made so much sense – finally! Following my own path! Getting out of my little town, living away from the inevitable comparisons with my twin sister. Then reality set in. It started creeping up on me and never stopped.

'Well, well, well, if it isn't our old friend, Señor Mango

Sorbet,' Cassie says. I look out towards the seafront and spot a couple of our regulars: a stylish, good-looking, well-groomed couple in their early fifties, who have taken to stopping by on their way home a few times in this first week alone.

'And his wife, Lady Red Plum,' I chime in.

'One scoop of mango sorbet, please!' says Señor Mango Sorbet, fishing in his back pocket for his wallet. 'And for the Mrs . . .'

Lady Red Plum says, 'I'll have—'

'A scoop of red plum?' Cassie interjects, grinning.

'You read my mind! Am I that predictable?!' The woman smiles and brushes her hair out of her eyes. A huge diamond ring glints on her finger.

'Not at all,' I reply. 'It's my favourite flavour too!'

They pay and thank us, wandering off licking their ice creams.

'Do you reckon people find it weird that we remember their orders?' Cassie asks me, as if struck by a horrible thought.

I consider it for a moment. 'I'm not sure . . . maybe people like feeling seen? And remembered?'

'Yeah. I mean, there are worse things to be remembered for.'

'We remember those two because they're so together.

So sure of themselves. Not just because they always order the same thing.'

'Yeah . . .' she agrees. 'Except . . . no one's really all that together, right? Everyone's got stuff going on. I wonder what their stuff is.'

Finally, six o'clock rolls around and it's time to close the stall. Mercifully the weekend shift belongs to Graham, an overzealous retiree who has discovered a second life as an ice-cream salesman, and Chelsea, who doesn't take it seriously at all, so Cassie and I are at liberty to hang up our aprons and indulge in a couple of pints.

'Where do you want to go?' Cassie asks. 'Crown or Lighthouse?'

What she's really asking is: what kind of night are we planning on having? There *are* other pubs in Weston Bay – lots in fact – but we generally just pinball between those two. The Lighthouse is run by my Uncle Michael, who takes his work sufficiently seriously that he's there almost every night of the week. He took it over with his husband, Mark, a couple of years ago and it's now a perfectly Instagram-ready haunt with cocktails, velvet seats, hanging planters and kitschy details. If we go to the Lighthouse it'll be a sedate evening under the watchful eye of Uncle Michael and/or Mark. But if we go to the Crown . . . anything could happen. It will be extreme summer evening vibes.

'Crown,' I say, decisively.

'Oh, so it's going to be *that* kind of night. I'm gonna save your "one new thing" until we get there, in that case.' Cassie smiles as she zips up the cash bag, ready for her parents to pick it up in a few minutes. 'See you at eight thirty?'

'See you there!' I blow her a kiss before starting my slow stroll home.

The man at the shellfish stand waves to me as I pass, and I let the Friday feeling infuse my wave back. Carl? Kyle? I don't even know his name, but Daisy and I went to primary school with his daughter Maisie and I guess no one forgets the twins. The waving was a ritual we started when I used to walk home from school in town and even though I disappeared for two years for college, we've picked it right back up again. And on the rare occasion I actually buy something there, like a styrofoam cup of cockles doused in vinegar and pepper, he always gives me a bigger cup than he charges me for. It's just one of the many threads that make up the fabric of my life here.

I know you're meant to hate the place you grow up, but I don't. Weston Bay is . . . fine. No, it's more than fine. Even in the winter when the place seems to go into hibernation, as the freezing wind whips up the sea and sends the spray right into your face . . . OK, that's not great. But on days like this I wouldn't change it for anything. Some of my fellow Westonians are walking in the fading light, taking pleasure in the sea air and the beauty of living here and now. I get out my phone and take a photo of the way the light is hitting the pier and glinting off the sea like glitter. I'll paint it next time I have a moment.

I'm barely through the front door before Daisy bounds down the stairs to ask me if I want to join her and her friend Erin to see some film about a genetically engineered crocodile tearing up LA. Alas, I have plans.

Daisy shrugs. 'I'm mostly going so I can see if that guy I like is there.'

'You mean you're not going for the genetically engineered crocodile?!' I ask in mock surprise.

'A little from column A, a little from column B.'

'I can't believe you two are abandoning your old mum on a Friday night!' Mum says, appearing at the top of the stairs like a meerkat from its hole.

I tilt my head skeptically. 'You're not *that* old . . .'

'Sweet of you to say. Anyway, I'm meeting Jade at the Lighthouse.' Mum grew up here too, and even though most of her friends have moved away, a few, like Jade, remain. Jade is always trying to get Mum to go out and meet guys. Something Daisy and I pretend to disapprove of but actually very much support. Especially since we're both moving out at the end of the summer. Maybe it's naive of me to think Mum will be bored without us, but also, maybe I'm right, and the thought of the cottage being empty and my bed not being slept in and most of my stuff being somewhere else so far away . . .

'Lily?' I realize Mum's been talking to me.

'Sorry?' I ask, breezily.

'I was just asking what you're up to tonight.'

'Oh, just going for a drink in town.'

'Have fun!' Mum says as she bounds out the door. She's pretty laid back as mums go, but she does like to know the bare minimum.

Daisy turns back to me. 'Who are you going with? Oh wait, I love this game. Let me guess . . . hmm,' she says, furrowing her brow in mock concentration. I involuntarily huff. 'Is it Cassie?'

'Is that a problem?' I ask wearily.

'No, it's just . . . you used to know *other people*. You used to have other friends! Now you never see them! When was the last time you saw Molly or Aminah from school, even?'

'I've seen them . . .' I haven't seen them. It's just that everything changed when I got to college. I started to feel freer. I hated my GCSEs because I had to take *so* many subjects I wasn't even good at and didn't care about, and then I got to college and was able to whittle them down to only things I was into. And it was the same with my friends,

I guess. There's nothing wrong with my friends from school, though – they're really cool girls. But when I met Cassie I just . . . didn't feel like I needed anyone else.

'I'm just worried that when you go to uni in September you won't be able to survive without her,' Daisy says, gently. It's like she's managed to read my mind even though I haven't really shared any of my fears with her. This is a twin thing I could do without. This unspoken psychic bond. This . . . knowability. It makes me feel predictable. 'It's like you've narrowed your focus on the world down to such a small area. And the world's going to get bigger really suddenly in a couple of months.'

'Fine, I'll text Molly from school and see if she wants to do something, if that'll make you feel reassured about my future,' I say, taking my phone out of my pocket and typing a text to my old friend asking if she's free this weekend. I might not actually *want* to meet up with her, but I can't only do the things I want to do. It's outside of my comfort zone! Therefore it must be worth my while! 'I'm going to get ready to meet Cassie at the Crown.'

'Wasn't it only a week ago I was trying to get you to come to the Crown with me, Sasha and Lou?' Daisy asks, a little accusatory.

'Yeah.' I shrug. 'I wasn't feeling like it. Enjoy the silly film! I hope you get to creep on your crush!' I pound up the stairs.

# CHAPTER THREE

On the one hand, we're only going to the Crown, but on the other hand, it's a Friday night so I should probably scrub up a little. Getting ready to go out is one of the only times I wish my sister and I were the same size: it would mean double the clothes. It's not as if I'm short of things to wear though, so I shouldn't complain. And it's one less thing for me to miss when I go to uni.

I settle on a cute black T-shirt dress with bare legs and trainers, and swipe on some mascara, bronzer and pinky-beige lipstick. Gotta let those freckles shine through! I run a paddle brush through my hair before throwing it down on the bed as if I'm not just going to have to move it when I return after a few pints.

As I pass the row of beautiful Georgian townhouses that run along the seafront with an unobstructed view of the water, I bathe in the warm glow of the lights coming from the living rooms. It reminds me of a Magritte painting with the sky still kind of bright and the buildings in shadow, with the exception of the illuminated windows. Suddenly, something about the encroaching darkness makes me quicken my pace.

As I approach the Crown, I see Cassie walking towards me from the opposite direction. One thing about us? We're *always* on time for everything.

'Hello angel!' Cassie greets me with a hug even though I only saw her a couple of hours ago. I hold her at arm's length, my hands on her shoulders, to look at her outfit. A grey linen sundress with wide straps and a square neckline which she's made herself, but looks like something discerning London ladies would pay top dollar for in one of the little boutiques at the 'cool' end of the high street.

'Perfection!' I yell, throwing my head back.

'Ugh, you say that like you don't always look absolutely perfect, you monster,' says Cassie, rolling her eyes, exasperated but loving it.

'It's true though! You've done it again. Your mind!' I say as we enter the raucous, sticky-floored pub. 'What a perfect Friday night it is.'

'Maybe we can even . . .' Cassie raises her eyebrows expectantly.

'Sit outside?' I finish. There is simply nothing Cassie loves more than a pub garden.

Cassie spins around and grabs me enthusiastically by the cheeks, holding my face in her hands. 'You know me so well!'

The garden, with its overhead heaters and twinkly lights, is one of the Crown's redeeming features, even if the benches are a little bit splintery.

'What do you want to drink?' I ask when we reach the bar.

'What do you think?' Cassie replies. She's right. I didn't need to ask.

'One pint of your cheapest lager for my friend here,' I say to the barman. 'And a vodka, lemon and lime, please.' I produce some cash from my purse but somehow it turns out to be even cheaper than I expected. Bless the Crown and all who drink in her.

As we make our way outside, we see a few girls from college sitting at a table in the neon glow of the slot machines. We wave but make no actual effort to go over and say hi.

'What's the name of the girl in the red top again?' Cassie asks as we sit down in a prime spot: with a wall to lean against and under a heat lamp in case it gets too chilly out here.

'The one in the pink top is . . . I want to say . . . Aisha? And the other one is Naomi? I think?'

'You really never forget anyone, do you?'

'It's one of my few natural talents,' I say, sipping my drink.

'One of *many*,' Cassie corrects. 'I know I'm going to sound mega old but . . . isn't it nice to sit down?'

I hoot with laughter. 'You sound *ancient*, but honestly I never appreciated the pure joy of sitting down until I started working at the ice-cream stand!'

'A blessing that we're both naturally drawn to sensible shoes.'

'Yes, but remember when sensible shoes nearly killed me?!'

'We wouldn't be here without your horrible injury,' Cassie says, taking another sip of her icy-cold beer. She shudders. 'Ugh, I remember the way you were *properly limping* on the first day of college. Who tries to break in Dr Martens on an already very stressful day? Thank god I carry plasters. I looked at you hobbling on your way to our first politics class and thought, *I must save her!*' Cassie clutches her chest dramatically.

'God, that was such a HUGE day for me. It was the first time I'd been separated from Daisy since, I guess, before we were even invented.' It was weird going from a tiny girls' school where I knew everyone, to taking the bus along to Seaforth for college. My school didn't offer A level art, so I couldn't really stay anyway. But being split up from Daisy for the first time in our lives was *really* weird. 'My shadow was gone! My Daisy-shaped shadow. My default person.'

I shake my head, remembering, a hollow feeling developing in the pit of my stomach at the thought of next year. Not just sitting in different classrooms a few miles away, but living properly separate lives.

'But then you got a new default person.' Cassie shrugs, casually.

I think, but don't say, *The coolest girl I'd ever seen*. A gold nose ring, cat-eye glasses, a bouncy twist-out in a deep side parting, a shiny gold backpack to match the art portfolio she had spray-painted gold and *always* wearing bright, bold patterns (clothes which I would later discover she made herself, because she's that cool). 'Real-life legend Cassie Palmer turned around from the row in front of me, wordlessly holding out a handful of plasters,' I say instead.

'Memories! What a saint I am.'

I don't say that after I'd put the plasters on the backs of my heels, covering up where the leather had rubbed the skin raw, I tried to focus on the introduction from Miss Sanderson, our Government and Politics teacher, but kept looking over Cassie's shoulder, realizing that whenever she wasn't taking notes, she was drawing. I guess for anyone else they would be doodles, but Cassie's were like tiny little sketches. Even though I was sitting a metre or so away, I could see that they were faithful renderings of people in the class. A page of notes surrounded by little faces. I wanted to know her.

'And the rest is history!' I say. I'd sidled up to her after the class to thank her, and to ask if she was going to be in my art class too, which I'd rightly assumed from the portfolio. We became so close so fast that I barely noticed the weeks slipping by and the fact that weekend after weekend would pass without me seeing my old friends from school. If I say she's not just my best friend but kind of my only friend, it sounds a bit sad, but it doesn't feel sad to me. Should I try to broaden my horizons? Probably. Would I rather not? Definitely.

Two rounds down, I leap to my feet as soon as our empty glasses hit the table. 'Another?'

'Well . . . it would be rude not to, wouldn't it?' Cassie says with a lopsided grin. She's cute when she's tipsy.

'So rude.'

I make my way to the bar and find myself queuing next to Aisha. 'Hey!'

'Oh, hey Lily! How are you? I haven't seen you in ages!' The music is too loud in here and we have to yell to make ourselves heard.

'Yeah, I dropped history for A level so I guess we wouldn't have any other classes together. But I'm fine! Trying to make the most of our last summer.' I shrug, somehow able to say 'last summer' without spiralling. 'How about you?'

'Yeah, all good thanks,' she says, wrapping her small hands precariously around three glasses of rosé. 'Are you here with . . . Callie?'

'Cassie,' I correct her.

'Cassie, that's right!' Aisha rolls her eyes at her own forgetfulness. 'I didn't know you two were still together.'

'What?' I furrow my brow, sure that I misheard her over the volume of the music and the Friday night crowd.

'It's nice you two are still together,' she enunciates clearly into my ear.

'Oh . . . we're not—'

'It was nice to see you! Better order before someone nicks your place.' And with that she's gone.

As the barman pours our drinks, I turn her words over in my head. Cassie and I are just friends, everyone knows that.

I slowly make my way back to the beer garden with the drinks. As I approach I realize Cassie isn't alone and my chest automatically tightens in defence. I can't be bothered to deal with random guys tonight, I just want to hang out with her. We normally get left alone and that's kind of how I like it.

'These gentlemen asked if they could join us on this table as the pub is so busy tonight,' Cassie says.

'Sure,' I say as gamely as I can manage, setting the glasses down and sizing up the invaders.

'This is Jack,' says Cassie, nodding to the guy opposite her, and he does a little salute as he sips his pint, caught slightly off-guard by the introduction. He seems fairly harmless, so I guess he can stay.

'Hello Jack, I'm Lily,' I say, taking my place next to Cassie. Jack's not bad-looking I guess – he's got some pretty stylish glasses and a mop of fair hair.

'And this is Cal,' Cassie says, gesturing towards the taller guy with dark hair who's texting someone furiously. He drops his phone on the table and looks up at me and just like that I'm *gone*. Oh no. He's beautiful. I can't focus on anything except the pounding in my chest. Cal smiles broadly and extends his hand towards me and I feel like my heart could melt. My insides are fizzy. What's happening to me?! I interrupt my gawping to look down at his hand and realize I'm meant to do something.

'Hello, Cal, I'm still Lily,' I say finally, taking his hand and shak-ing it. 'My, what a strong grip you have.'

'So,' says Cal. 'How do you two occupy yourselves?' As he speaks I realize he has a strong New Zealand accent. It makes me smile involuntarily.

'We are saleswomen,' I say with a flourish of my hand, like a game show hostess showing off some exciting prizes.

'Oh, really?' Cal says, raising his eyebrows, a light dancing in his eyes. 'What do you sell?'

'Cassie here is an ice-cream heiress.' I shrug, nonchalantly. She swats at my arm.

'Heiress!' Cassie dissolves into laughter.

'This is not just any Cassie. This is Cassie Palmer, heiress to the Palmer's Ices *fortune*, I tell you,' I say, banging my hand on the table for emphasis.

'I had no idea we were in the company of an heiress, Jack! Of all the tables we could have sat at . . .' Cal shakes his head slowly, marvelling. Jack just smiles warmly.

'So you're not from around here?' I ask.

Cal smiles and my stomach does a little flip. I remember to check in with my face muscles to ensure I'm not grinning wildly. 'I'm from as far away from here as it's possible to be.'

'And you, Jack?'

'Not me,' he says quietly, looking a little embarrassed. 'I'm only from Seaforth.' He gives off a calmer, less exuberant energy than the gorgeous Cal.

'Nothing wrong with that!' Cassie says, clinking her glass against his.

I was sceptical about having our evening interrupted by two random dudes, but they're kind of great. We chat and laugh and every so often I catch Cal's eye and part of me wonders if he's looking at me the way I think he's looking at me. I want to text Cassie under the table to ask if I'm imagining things, but every time I get my phone ready in my hands, I'm distracted by the chemistry between Cassie and Jack. And then Cal says something brilliant and I forget about texting Cassie all together.

After a while, Jack surveys the empty glasses on the table. 'Another?'

I sigh theatrically. 'Go on then.' Cassie and Cal aren't going to turn down another either.

As soon as Jack has rounded up the glasses and headed for the bar, Cassie reaches across the table and gently touches Cal's hand in a motion that briefly makes me burn with a jealousy so surprising I don't know where it comes from.

'Would you excuse us for just a moment?' Cassie says, smiling sweetly, retracting her hand. 'Lady business.'

'I wouldn't dream of getting between you two and lady business.' He sits back and puts his hands behind his head in a pose of extreme relaxation.

Cassie takes me by the arm and drags me to the bathroom. I wonder if some other girl is going to come and talk to him while we're gone. It all seems a bit too good to be true.

'Well, well, well,' she says, pulling the bathroom door closed behind me, 'what do we have here?'

'Uhhh, too soon to tell.' Cassie is all systems go but I'm much too sceptical about . . . well, guys. The way the world works. 'But . . . I guess maybe I kind of felt like maybe Cal was checking me out?'

'Oh yeah, *maybe!*' Cassie's face is disbelieving yet deeply imploring. 'You shouldn't be so surprised! It's literally not that surprising that two cute guys would like us.'

'Would like *you!* That wouldn't be surprising,' I say, realizing as soon as it comes out of my mouth how whiny and pathetic it sounds.

She looks at me, distinctly unimpressed. 'Come on. It's not like it's a breeze for me trying to meet people in this weird, sneaky, racist little world.' My stomach clenches with embarrassment.

'Yeah, you're right, I'm sorry,' I say, looking down at my feet. 'It's just very easy for me to fixate on all the ways I'm not good enough.'

'I can't let you talk about my best friend like this. Nope.'

'But just think about it. It's not like I ever have much luck with guys, right?'

'Only because they're invariably pathetic worms who don't deserve the time of day. These two seem alright!'

'I guess I'm just a bit put off by my track record,' I say, thinking of the few times I've been out with this guy I met at a party. A fumble in a dark bathroom. Boring conversation. No chemistry. No joy. Just going through the motions.

'That's the past! This is the present! And the future! Besides, Daisy isn't here!' It's like she can read my mind.

'So stop coming up with excuses! There's no need for them! This is the Lily Rose Show. No Daisy to speak of!' Cassie says, clapping her hands together decisively. 'I've got a concept for you.'

'Hit me,' I say, trying to sound confident so Cassie doesn't come away from this with the belief I'm *completely* pathetic.

'Today's new thing,' she says, breathing deeply, closing her eyes and bringing her hands to a serene prayer stance in front of her chest, 'is to not sabotage this. To let yourself experience this to its fullest potential. To not force yourself to drop out of the running. How does that sound?'

'Scary,' I say, grimacing. 'But I can't argue with the Law of New Things.' Half of me is nervous about daring to dream that someone like Cal might be into me. Half of me is excited that someone's given me the licence to dream.

'That's my girl.'

'Well,' I say, smiling, 'I ain't no one else's.'

Cassie's looking in the mirror over the sink, applying a deep berry lipstick. 'Jack's kind of cute, right? I'm not completely losing it, am I?'

'He's definitely cute,' I reassure her, though he isn't a patch on Cal if you ask me.

She rubs her lips together and drops her lipstick back in

her bag. 'Good. This is a fun little twist and I'm here for it. Let's get to it.'

When we get back to the table, Jack and Cal are huddled in conversation and our drinks are waiting for us. I let it all in. I let myself sneak glances at Cal as we drink and chat. I let myself maybe flirt with him a little. I let my leg brush against his under the table. I don't take myself out of the running.

And when Cassie announces it's her round and that she's going to get us all another drink whether we like it or not, Jack leaps to his feet and trots after her like a lovesick puppy. Leaving me deliciously alone with Cal.

We sit in weighted silence for a moment before Cal stands up and walks round to my side of the table, to Cassie's vacated seat. Next to me. 'This is a fun night,' he says, looking out at the pub garden. He's so close I can hear him breathing. Feel the warmth of his body. 'I wasn't sure what it was going to be like because I dragged Jack out post-brutal dumping, but he seems to be hitting it off with your friend.'

'Yeah, I guess,' I say, slightly unsure. Whatever was going on between Cassie and Jack, she usually needs a little more convincing than just talking to someone over a couple of drinks. She's normally much more fussy – I feel like maybe she's only going along with the Jack thing to encourage me to try it out with Cal. It's unlikely to stick.

'And . . . I think you're pretty great,' he says. My heart leaps, my brain unsure what to do with this directness. I blush.

'Well, who doesn't?' I say with a confidence I'm trying on for size.

'I think you're pretty great and also just . . . pretty,' Cal says, turning to face me and moving a little closer. He's got a clean, warm, cottony scent. Nothing artificial, no cheap body spray, just himself. I can't help but grin. It's not like I *never* meet guys, but it's not something I take for granted. Most boys my age are kind of pathetic about the way girls look and sometimes that makes it hard for me to fully *own* my body, even though I know there's nothing wrong with me.

'Would it be OK if I . . .' Cal pauses. 'Kissed you?'

I let out a small involuntary gasp that I hope isn't audible over the noise of the Crown on a Friday. But I start to feel reassured: he likes me. I am in control, I tell myself. 'Yes, that would be . . . more than OK.'

He brings his hand to the back of my head and slowly, deliberately, kisses me. Soft and warm and comfortable but exciting, too. We pull apart before kissing again and in the brief seconds between kisses when I open my eyes and look at him I think, *Wow, yes, you really are gorgeous.*

'Do you understand how good-looking you are?' I hear a voice say as I'm gazing into his eyes. My hand flies to my mouth, eyes wide in horror, as I realize the voice was *mine*. No! No! No! I was meant to be in control! I feel my cheeks burning but he's not backing away in fear.

'Ha!' Cal crows in delight. 'You're not so bad yourself. You're all . . . I don't know, kind of serious-looking? I like it. And those freckles.'

I don't say anything, just gulp down whatever idiotic thought I was about to come out with next. 'Wow,' I finally manage, quietly. Suddenly emboldened by his words, I turn my face up towards him and kiss him again.

But in the back of my mind, something in me hopes that Cassie doesn't come back while we're kissing.

Finally, we pull apart and I can't help but let out a nervous laugh, covering my face with my hands so he can't see how much I'm smiling, until finally Cassie and Jack return from the bar with two drinks each. Cassie raises her eyebrows at me like she knows what's happened.

I pass the rest of the evening in a daze. I can't quite get my head around the fact that Cal went *for me*. In a whole pub full of girls. A whole town full of girls. He has a perfect smile, high, wide cheekbones, an easy confidence. And he went for me. First. Not second. First. I never thought it could be so easy to meet someone who's not freaked out about my body.

After midnight, a scrawny teen boy prowls through the pub garden collecting glasses and telling us to move inside and drink up. Grudgingly we comply. As we walk inside, I realize Cassie and Jack have hung back, and when I look back over my shoulder, I see their bodies pressed together under the heat lamp, in a drunken, messy kiss. Huh, Cassie must be more drunk than I thought. I reach out for Cal's hand. He smiles warmly.

'So . . . can I get your number?' Cal asks shyly as we sit in an empty booth inside to finish our drinks.

I sigh nonchalantly, holding my hand out in front of me and examining my nails, as if gorgeous guys ask me this every day. 'Oh, I suppose so,' I say, glowing on the inside while trying not to blush. I dictate the number to him and he drop-calls me so I have his.

'Not to be too forward, but . . . do you want to meet up tomorrow night?' Something about Cal makes me feel so good. He's kind. And cute. So of course I say yes.

Before long, Cassie and Jack make an appearance.

'So, where to now?' Cassie asks as we step out into the mild July night.

'Are you serious? I'm exhausted after a whole day's work!' I gawp at her.

'Yeah, I'm pretty tired,' says Cal, smiling. 'But I'll see you tomorrow, Lily?'

'Yeah, tomorrow,' I reply.

'We could always go to the Lighthouse if you don't want to go home, Cass?' Jack asks optimistically. No one calls her Cass, not even me. For some reason, she doesn't correct him. 'I think it's open later than the Crown. Or we could try one of the old man pubs down the high street? Or maybe we could go see what's on at work?'

'Oh yeah, I just realized, after all that – we don't even know what you guys do?' Cassie furrows her brow and takes a sip from the rose-gold water bottle she keeps in her bag ('Gotta stay hydrated!' she likes to remind me).

'We,' says Cal, throwing his arm around Jack just as I take a sip from the water bottle Cassie's offered me, 'work at the Coronet.'

I splutter out a spray of water and pretend I was overcome by a sudden urge to cough. 'The cinema?' I ask, even though I know that it's definitely the cinema. *Blue eyes. Cool accent. Works at the cinema.* Oh. No. Oh no no no.

'Yeah,' says Jack, misinterpreting my reaction as some kind of judgement on his work. 'It's not so bad. Tonight I got to sit in on a screening.'

I have done a bad thing.

'While I had no such luck and was stuck on the main till

with a broken drinks machine. Friday night's meant to be a big night for neon frozen beverages!' Cal throws his hands in the air in defeat.

There's no two ways about it: Cal is definitely Daisy's crush.

'Can you get us in for free?' Cassie asks optimistically, but I'm not really listening. Daisy likes Cal. She's been after him for so long. But he's here . . . with me. I can't stop turning it all over in my mind. He chose me, not Daisy. Maybe he didn't know that Daisy's been flirting with him all year? Or maybe he does, and he would just rather go out with me? I can't possibly still go out with him, right? WHAT IF DAISY FOUND OUT?!

Jack shrugs. 'Why not! So, what do you say, Lighthouse for one more?'

I give Cassie a look – he's keen.

'Sure,' Cassie says with a grin. 'I'll text you, Lily!'

With that, they're off. I'm left standing here with that head-spinning want for Cal, that tug of guilt that he's *Daisy's crush,* and that tiny little streak of pride that he chose *me.*

'Well . . . I'll see you tomorrow, right?' Cal says, taking my hand and wrapping it around his waist like he knew I would be too shy to do it myself.

'Right,' I mumble, looking into his eyes. One last kiss

before I go. Just one more. I'll figure this whole thing out when I'm more sober.

The lights are on at home as I walk up the path. I open the door gently and close it behind me almost silently, slipping my shoes off so I can pad up the stairs undetected.

'Lily!' I hear Daisy whisper sharply from the kitchen as I'm reaching the top of the stairs. I pretend I don't hear her. I brush my teeth and look at myself in the mirror and through the guilt and the white toothpaste foam, a smile breaks through.

# CHAPTER FOUR

I wake up feeling slightly hungover with that classic foggy headache and dry mouth. I definitely can't keep this up all summer. I roll over and check my phone, flicking through the confusing memories of last night on Cassie's Instagram story. Just a few pictures from before Cal and Jack joined us. I put my phone back on charge and snuggle into my duvet. That stomach-jolt of joy at the sight of Cal's smile . . . the memory of that kiss. I feel a rush of excitement and then a pang of guilt when I hear the short vibration of my phone, and without even looking at it I feel sure it's Cal. I pick it back up. An unknown number. It must be him.

> Fish + chips tonight? 7 at the good place? Just promise me you won't be a typical Brit and make me say 'fish and chips' because you think my accent is silly!

I know where he means. Even though it's a seaside town and there are loads of places to eat fish and chips, there's only one that's good. Really good. Crunchy, crispy, golden kind of good. Fish that's structurally flaky but somehow still juicy kind of good. Chips that are fluffy in the middle and fried to perfection on the outside kind of good. It makes you wonder how anyone could get it wrong.

I instantly start typing my reply, unable to conceal my enthusiasm. But then . . . I think it through. A cloud of anxiety settles over me. The thought of going out with Daisy's crush is a strange new world, but surely she deserves to know? If he really is — whisper it — interested in me, I should tell her so she doesn't spend the rest of the summer hanging around the cinema waiting for her chance to talk to him. She's my *twin*! Maybe now's the time our twin telepathy will come in handy and I won't have to tell her at all. Or maybe that means I *do* have to tell her because she'll definitely guess otherwise.

But also . . . it's only one little date. It might come to nothing, and what's the point of causing trouble with Daisy over one date? Maybe he'll be a horrible misogynist or announce he hates all art! Then there's no need to tell her and no need to make things awkward and difficult before we go to uni. Anyway, he'll probably realize that society is right and he's much too good for me and that'll be the end of it. Or maybe he'll actually notice Daisy at the Coronet and then this whole thing can unfold the way everyone would expect it to, right?

I guess in that case . . . I should make hay while the sun shines. Enjoy it while it lasts. Enjoy being wanted, uncomplicatedly. Enjoy the attention of someone smart and compassionate enough to see things on their own terms, their view unclouded by beauty standards based on ideas that should have been thrown in the bin centuries ago. That's it. I'll go on one tiny little date, and if it goes well enough, I'll tell Daisy then. Finally, I reply.

I'll be there!

At that moment, Daisy bursts into my room like a snotty tornado, sniffing horribly. 'Lily!' she wails. Oh god, have I been found out so soon? What kind of whisper network is going on in this town?! 'I'm sorry, but I couldn't wait any longer and it's your fault anyway because you always leave the hay-fever medicine in your room as if I don't need to use it too,' she fumes, foraging around on my dressing table for the white box of antihistamines. Phew. Hay-fever. We are equally afflicted. I just routinely forget to leave the communal medicine in a communal location.

'And good morning to you, twin sister of mine!' I throw my arms up triumphantly as she locates the medicine.

Daisy rests a tablet on her tongue and sits down on my bed, reaching for a glass of last night's water. She downs it and grimaces as she realizes it's hours old.

'You'll feel better in no time,' I say, taking one myself. I pick up my phone again and text Cassie.

> Hope you got home ok!

Alive and well. Last night was fun!
Maybe we can DOUBLE DATE!!!!

I guess that means she's planning on seeing Jack again.

> Right now I'm focusing on a SINGLE DATE
> and I'm already stressed about what to wear
> so can you plsssssssssss be my stylist later?

Omg I literally thought you would
never ask. I'll FaceTime you like 6?

'Did you have fun last night?' Daisy asks, stroking Crystal who has padded her way onto the bed and is sitting in the hollow of Daisy's crossed legs.

'Yeah, it was good. Just normal. Just me and Cassie at the pub,' I say, shrugging. 'How about you? Was the shark film good? And by "good" I mean, like, in any way watchable or even vaguely entertaining?'

'For your information, it wasn't a shark, it was a crocodile. Sharks are very passé. And besides, the film was just a convenient excuse!' I feel relieved she hasn't mentioned seeing Cal. 'I saw my crush!' Damn.

'Oh yeah?' I ask, remaining carefully casual.

'Yeeeees.' She smiles, raising her eyebrows and running a finger through Crystal's fur. 'He definitely smiled at me.'

'Are you sure he doesn't just smile at everyone?' I say, thinking of his generally sunny and charming nature.

'Well, no, of course I'm not.' Daisy rolls her eyes. 'But I'm not completely stupid, I can tell what's going on. And I felt like there was some kind of connection, you know?'

'You're probably right!' I say. When I think about it, it's not out of the question that if Cal likes me he could also be making eyes at my sister. It's actually quite likely, in fact, since everyone seems to imply that I'm the inferior copy of her. But I can't think like that. I have to just . . . live in the moment.

'Maybe I am. I think I'm going to ask for his number next time I see him . . .' Daisy gets up and starts prowling around the room, surveying my stuff, looking at the pictures on the walls, most of which I've drawn or painted, as if she hasn't been in here a thousand times before.

'Godspeed,' I say, nodding sagely and hoping my cheeks aren't as red as they feel. I have a horrible vision of her asking him out at the cinema in front of her friends after hyping herself up to talk to him for months, only to get rejected. As much as I want him for myself, the thought of that makes me feel sick for her. I should say something. I should at least try to save her possible embarrassment. But how?

Daisy catches a glimpse of herself in the full-length mirror leaning against the wall. She stands at an angle, craning her neck. 'Do you think my thighs have got smaller?'

I make sure my face reads 'unimpressed' in case Daisy's glancing in my direction, but inside I'm squirming with discomfort. Any time she says something like this it reminds me she's looking at me with exactly the same gaze.

She runs a hand over them proudly. 'I think they have. Definitely.'

She resumes her prowl. That interlude probably meant nothing to her but I'll be thinking about it all day. Wondering if Daisy looks at my body the way she looks at hers.

'This one's my favourite,' she says suddenly, breaking me out of my thoughts. She bends slightly to look at a picture just below eye-level.

'The watercolour of Gran's garden?'

'Yeah.'

'That's your favourite of all the stuff I've done?' I ask, a little incredulously. It's just a watercolour the size of a postcard, faithfully replicating the layout, the flowers, the way the light hits the garden in the afternoon.

'Yeah,' Daisy says, stepping back to survey it in context.

'And of all the stuff on this wall as well.'

'You know there are paintings on there by, like, real people? Like Georgia O'Keeffe and Lee Krasner,' I say, smiling.

'I'm not saying it's better than those paintings, I'm just saying I like it more. Isn't art supposed to be subjective?' Daisy huffs, and I feel sorry for teasing her. She's only being kind. 'I don't know what "better" even means, all I can tell you is that it's my favourite thing that I see here.'

'Well, thank you . . .' I mutter.

'Anyway, I gotta bounce. My shift at the garden centre starts in an hour.'

'Don't have too much fun,' I say as she heads out.

She stops at the door and turns back to look at the room. 'You really do paint the things you love so well. It's like you bring out something in them that makes people see how you see things. I guess when you go to uni, you'll find a whole bunch of new stuff to love and you'll paint those too. Maybe I'll like those more than the painting of Gran's garden . . . but I doubt it.' And with that, she leaves.

I sit on my bed, a little lump in my throat. It's weird having someone in your life who understands you perfectly, whether you like it or not.

Will I have time to paint or even just draw when I'm at university in September? And even if I have time, will I have space? Where would I do it? And what would be the point if I'm studying art history anyway? I'll probably have essays to write and things to do. The reading list is as long as my arm so maybe I'll just stop painting as soon as I leave home and never do it again. I thought I would feel inhibited if I went to the same university as Daisy, but it's possible that she motivates me in ways I might not motivate myself.

I lay back on top of the covers and try to think about what my life will look like by the end of the summer. No Daisy, no Mum, no cottage, no sea. No Cassie. Everything has been so solidly the same for so long that I don't know what different will feel like. Maybe I should have stuck to the original plan and gone to uni with Daisy because then at least I would have her. But I can't think about that now. I can't think about how stupid it was for me to decide that everyone else was right, and that I *needed* to be independent before thinking through everything that meant leaving behind.

And it's happening again. Something dark is swirling around in my brain and clutching at my heart. I can feel heat rising to my head and tingling in my hands, my breath catching in my throat. I sit up on my bed and try to breathe deeply to steady myself. It feels like there's an elephant sitting on my chest and covering my mouth. I'm trapped inside a bubble with no air. I want to text Cal and cancel seeing him later but I don't want to let this thing win. I'm just sick of it flaring up and crashing into my day like a . . . well, an elephant. I just need to ride it out. Not let it get the better of me. Not let it ruin my whole day. Shove it to the side until the next time.

Desperate to focus my mind on something other than everything, I stick my hand under my bed and pull out my small sketchbook and the clanging tin of soft pencils. I take a deep breath and look out of the window. I draw, in big, gestural strokes at first, the view of the garden of the house behind ours, over the hedge. And then I move up to the back of their house and sketch the outline of the building and then the windows and doors and then the bricks and the windowpanes and the creeping green-black ivy. Of course, I can't make it green-black with my steely graphite pencils but I can darken it, add depth where there's a short little shadow of the house projecting itself onto the patio. I can control this picture. Whether it's good or bad, lifelike or unrecognizable. It's my work, I invented it. And that gives me a degree of calm, which is exactly what I need right now. Focus on the page, not on what's inside my head. Not on the date tonight.

Cassie FaceTimes me at six o'clock on the dot.

'I'm here, babe, what do you need?' she asks as she settles into a comfy position on her bed, leaning against her headboard and giving me her full attention.

'Outfit advice.' I hold up my first suggestion, a tight black T-shirt and ripped jeans.

'Aren't you gonna put it on?'

'Alright then,' I say, flipping the phone over so she can't see me change.

'Oi! It's dark in here!' I can hear her saying through the phone's speaker as I put the outfit on.

I hold the front-facing camera at arm's length to show her before resting it against a pile of books to liberate my hands. 'It's a good start,' she says, 'but I'm feeling like I want *cute* for you, like I want *romantic* for you, you know? This is quite sexy, which is obviously hot, but I just feel like romance is the one right now.'

'Uhhh . . .' I say, rummaging through the coat hangers in my wardrobe.

'What about that?' Cassie asks. 'That yellow thing!'

'This?' I pull out a lemon-yellow tea dress that I like to wear with my beaten-up (formerly) white trainers.

'Extremely *Beauty and the Beast* with your dark hair,' Cassie says, nibbling on a Dorito.

'An inspired suggestion,' I say, trying it on. *Huh*, I think, checking myself out in my full-length mirror. *Not too bad.*

I hold the phone up again. 'My mind!' Cassie yelps. 'This is the one!'

'I think you're right, you know! Ugh, where would I be without you?'

'You'd be just fine, I promise. Anyway, how are you feeling? Confident? Dare I say . . . sexy?' Cassie asks, optimistically.

I let out a sigh and flop onto the bed. 'I don't know, man . . . I'm nervous!'

'You already know he likes you!'

'That's the weird part – at least if he was being kinda cagey, kinda meh, I would know what to do with it. I have this horrible feeling it's some kind of elaborate prank,' I say, my anxiety overriding the knowledge that Cal has been nothing but kind and forthcoming. Not to mention *hot*.

'That would be a frankly bizarre amount of effort for a prank, mate.'

'I guess . . . he doesn't really seem like he would do that, does he?'

'Nope. And more importantly, he is not too good for you! This all makes perfect sense! It only *doesn't* make sense if you believe that everything narrow-minded people say is true.'

'I've been brainwashed. It *is* brainwashing, isn't it? This whole thing. This belief that some people are, like, *better* than others,' I say.

'You know it! You're literally one hundred per cent

prepared for this date: banging outfit, sparkling smile, and extremely keen boy who also happens to be extremely hot. Now, sort your life out and go show Daisy what you're wearing for that final smidgen of approval.'

I'm on the verge of telling Cassie about Cal being Daisy's crush, but I hold back. 'Daisy's out,' I say with a shrug. I feel like she wouldn't approve of my date this evening if she knew Cal was Daisy's crush. I know she wouldn't.

'Well you can show off when she's back. Don't worry so much! You're going to have fun and do today's new thing: go on a date with someone you *actually like*,' she urges before we say our goodbyes, frantic kisses sent towards the screen. Yeah, I guess that would be a new thing. Or would not telling Cassie about Cal be the 'new thing'? Oh god.

As soon as we hang up I realize that I don't know what to do about a jacket and in the space of one second my mind flips through a choose-your-own-adventure story. Hear me out: even though it's a hot summer day, as soon as the sun goes down it gets cold. So I don't want to be cold. But if I take a jacket, that will mean I have no excuse to do that cute-romantic-girl thing of taking *his* jacket, should he offer it. But also, what if all this happens and I take his jacket and *obviously* it doesn't fit? But also, it's not like he doesn't know I'm fat, so if he *did* give me his jacket I could just casually drape it over my shoulders . . . wow,

64

I'm really getting in deep with all of this. No jacket.

As if I haven't thought *quite* enough about my date outfit choices, I'm about to pick up a tube of red lipstick to swipe over my lips when I pause and wonder if he'll take that as a signal that I don't want to kiss him. I go for the sweet beigey-pink that makes my lips seem even fuller, look in the mirror, and feel genuinely happy with what I see.

I pick up my phone and, stomach churning, save Cal's number under 'C'. Just in case Daisy sees it. I wonder if that makes it look even more suspicious . . . but I can't risk it. Well, I guess that's tipped me over into straight-up lying. Not something I ever thought I'd do with Daisy. But just one date – then I'll deal with it. There probably won't be anything to deal with. It's just one date and that'll be the end of it.

'Lily!' Mum calls from the corridor, before entering my room. 'This book is actually really good, I— Well don't you look nice!'

She's holding yet another thriller in her hand. She will literally read anything as long as it has an element of suspense, and then she complains about how there are no good thrillers anymore and then she goes and buys another one.

I deflect again. 'I'd heard that book was good!'

'I mean you can never tell until the end,' she says, effectively distracted, 'but this one bodes well. I don't think it's going to turn out that a ghost was the murderer!' Daisy and I have rarely seen our mum more furious than when she read her most unsatisfying thriller ever, something she refers to often and with great bitterness.

'I don't know if me and Daisy could live through that again, let alone you.'

'So what are you up to today? Plans with Cassie?' she asks. 'I love that dress on you!'

'Thanks, Mum. No, not today . . . um . . .' I realize I haven't quite processed it myself yet. The concept of going on a date. It feels faintly embarrassing to make something of it, even though I'm used to sharing stuff with my mum. Plus, I've got to make sure nothing too interesting-sounding gets back to Daisy. I go for vagueness. 'I'm meeting someone tonight.' Of course, there is nothing so interesting as vagueness when it's phrased like this.

Mum snaps her book shut with a big grin. '*Someone* is a very non-specific word!'

'Just someone I met last night when I was out with Cassie . . .' I say, blushing. 'We're only going to the good fish and chips place, it's nothing serious. Don't worry about it, Mum.'

'I'm not worried! I'm delighted! Not that there's

anything wrong with leaving things a bit later,' she adds, hastily.

'It's not like I'm forty!' I say, defensively. Daisy has had various boyfriends on and off for the past few years, and our mum has always remained very hands-off about the fact that I haven't. Which I appreciate. I don't need to be reminded. I don't particularly want to do a deep dive into my psyche or hear someone tell me my romantic life would just magically improve if I was thin or whatever. I like my body despite the fact that everyone else constantly compares me with Daisy and then lets me know when they find me lacking. It's nice that my mum has just let me be.

'No, of course not.' She rolls her eyes at me. 'I'm not going to be bugging you about it, don't worry. I just think it's nice.'

I sigh. 'Thank you.'

'And is this somebody . . .' She raises her eyebrows as if she wants me to finish her sentence, but I don't actually know what she's asking. 'A . . . boy?'

'Yes,' I say.

'Well, I don't want to assume! It would be worse if I assumed!'

'I guess,' I say with a shrug, feeling uncomfortable about the whole conversation now. But no time for that! I've got to stay focused on the task at hand. A date! A whole date!

A real, actual date, like in the movies. Not loitering by the war memorial drinking cans. Me, going on a real date. It almost sounds too good to be true. 'Hey, Mum . . .' Daisy would maybe find my Summer of New Things silly, but I feel like my mum would get it.

'Yes?'

'I'm doing this . . . thing. I'm trying to do something new every day. Not necessarily something huge. But just . . . something. A Summer of New Things.' I blush. It sounds a bit crazy when I say it out loud.

'Oh, I love that!' Mum says, stroking my hair. She sighs. 'It's the time for it, isn't it? Big changes around here.' She looks around, as if she's trying to figure out what it'll look like with me and Daisy gone, all our stuff gone, the house all quiet.

'Yeah.' I smile weakly, as if I think it's a good thing. An exciting thing.

'I've been thinking, maybe I should try something new too . . .' Mum says. 'Maybe try to meet someone. Maybe it's time to give it a go. Maybe it can be my Summer of New Things, too.'

'I like this for you!'

'I like it for me, too. Now, go, go, go! I don't want to hold you up!'

\*

I'm barely at the end of the road when Daisy rounds the corner on her way home from work and almost knocks me over.

'Huh! You look nice!' Daisy exclaims, only a little incredulously before squinting at my lips. 'Is that my Peachy Cream lipstick you're wearing?'

'No, actually, it's mine! It's Blossom Rose, anyway.' For the sake of not getting stressed out before my date with Cal, I resist the urge to ask why me looking nice has to have something to do with her and can't be, you know, an organic phenomenon.

'Fine, but if it's not there when I get back there's going to be trouble. Where are you off to, anyway?'

'Nowhere.' I shrug nonchalantly, before realizing that 'nowhere' is not a satisfying answer and I will absolutely have to give her something. 'Just meeting an old friend I bumped into at the pub last night.'

'Oooh! A non-Cassie friend! I approve.' She gasps, so delighted that she's verging on patronizing. 'You'll have to tell me all about her when you're home, I don't want to detain you.' And with that, she gives me an encouraging pat on the butt and runs off home.

I don't feel good about skirting around the truth.

As I walk into town to meet Cal at Little Lane Fish Shop, a Dickensian-looking structure on a pedestrianized street far too tiny for cars to get down, I realize that I'm excited rather than nervous about seeing him. I thought I had to be nervous because it's a date, but really I'm just looking forward to it. I know we're going to have a good time.

I see him before he sees me, which gives me an opportunity to scope out how he's looking. Which is, generally speaking, even cuter than I remember from last night. He's wearing a teal-coloured check shirt like a lumberjack and black jeans with trainers.

'Hey!' Cal greets me a little shyly, like he can't tell whether he's meant to hug me or kiss me or both or neither so we end up doing this hideous hug-kiss-handshake.

'Hey,' I say, trying to let the cringe subside. 'Let me get this? Just tell me what you want and I'll sort it.'

Cal frowns at me. 'Are you sure?'

'Yeah! I'm feeling generous today,' I tell him, infused with the good feeling he seems to provoke. Besides, it's only fish and chips.

I go in to order, and I realize the guy behind the counter was one of a group of guys from the boys' school next to ours who Daisy and I would sometimes walk to school with.

'Hi Sam! Cute little hat you've got there,' I say, gesturing to the white hairnet keeping his dark curls under control.

'Oh, hey! Yeah, it's, uh, extremely next season.' He smiles, baring his metallic braces. 'It's been a while!'

I place our order and lean against the counter while Sam scoops chips into a bag.

'How's Daisy?'

'She's fine,' I say, although I'm really trying not to think about Daisy too much this evening. 'Still constantly busy, always dashing off somewhere.' I stare, fascinated, at the devilish-red saveloy sausages under the counter. 'Hey, are you going to uni in September?' I look up at Sam.

'Uh, yeah,' he says, dabbing at his forehead with the crook of his elbow. 'Politics at Edinburgh.' Before I can congratulate him, he asks, 'What's Daisy going to be up to then?'

'Physics at Bristol, and I'm—'

'That's cool.' He cuts me off, nodding sagely as he puts the paper bags into a thin plastic bag. 'She was always into cool shit like that.'

'I guess . . .' I say.

'That'll be ten pounds eighty, please,' Sam says, ringing it up on the till.

I hand over a note and a coin. 'Thanks.'

'Say hi to Daisy from me! Would be good to see her before we go to uni!'

'Sure,' I say, dropping my change into a tip jar even though I feel like Sam should be tipping *me* for that conversation. Thank you so much for reminding me that

Daisy is the beautiful and fascinating one and I'm just . . . well, I'm just me.

I step outside and Cal's gorgeous, kind, smiling face is the breath of fresh air I need right now. Sam's idiocy would probably have bothered me more if I wasn't on an actual date with Actual Cal. He takes the bag from me and lets it swing gently as we walk, me stealing glances at him and yes, every time, he is as cute as I remember. We make our way to the seafront, settling on a bench near the end of the pier, and look out over the sea.

'Tell me about you,' Cal says.

My mind goes blank as I wrack my brains for anything interesting. 'I paint?' I venture, somehow turning the thing I'm most passionate about into a question, as though I'm asking him if it's interesting information.

'Cool! What do you paint?' He seems genuinely enthused, which is *delightful*.

'Landscapes and seascapes. Places. I'm interested in colour and how you can create form with it and I always feel like nature is a good place to look for those meeting points,' I say, and then I blush. 'Sorry, I always find it really weird talking about my painting, like it's embarrassing or something.'

'I bet your work's amazing. Do you want to paint my portrait?' He forms a frame around his face with his hands and furrows his brow seriously.

'Ha!'

'What? I'm not a good enough subject for you?'

'No, it's not that . . . I just don't really do people.'

'No?' He looks surprised.

'I used to,' I reply. I chew my lip for a moment. 'But there was something intimidating about painting portraits, like I would reveal something of myself in how I painted someone else. Like anyone who looked at the painting would find out something about me that I didn't intend to share.' I'm taken aback by my own words. I hadn't planned on saying something so personal but it just came out. I glance at Cal out of the corner of my eye. He looks thoughtful, not put off.

'I get that,' he says, handing me the box of fish and unfurling the bag of chips. 'We're always looking for autobiography in people's work. Projecting things onto it.'

'Especially women's work,' I add, putting my hand in the bag and gently grazing Cal's hand as he pulls it out.

'Yeah, for sure.' He looks at me straightforwardly. He's not interested in playing any games.

'What's New Zealand like?' I ask, before nibbling my chip.

'It's amazing, some of it looks like another planet. Very green. Lots of sheep. Lots of rain,' he says. He looks kind of wistful and nostalgic. 'But it feels kind of small. I mean, I guess it is kind of small. I just wanted to see something else. Meet other people. See what life is like somewhere else.'

'Specifically Weston Bay?'

'Ha! No, not quite that specific. I was working in a bar in London for a while but I wanted to try somewhere less . . . hectic before I go back. And it's always nice to be by the sea, isn't it?'

'Yes,' I say, looking out across the water. It almost comes out like a sigh. The sand, the sea and the glowing sunset sky are forming hazy, indistinct bars of colour, in the style of a Mark Rothko painting. It really is so beautiful. And somehow Cal manages to look so at home, right in the middle of it. 'How long do you reckon you'll stay here?'

'Probably just until the end of the summer,' he says. 'Jack helped me find a short-term let in a flat with a couple of other guys. I'm only responsible for that until the end of September.' Even less reason to mention this to Daisy. A classic summer romance with a clear expiry date. At least that's one thing I don't have to worry about losing when I go to uni. *Don't think about it, don't think about it, stay in the moment*, I tell myself. I can't have my fear of going away polluting tonight as well. 'I should probably return to my real life, you know?' he says. 'I can't put it off forever. Starting the rest of my life.' He runs his hands through the thick sweep of dark hair that's falling over his eyebrow.

And that little thought that just keeps coming back rears its ugly head once again: why is he bothering with me? If he could have Daisy, why not have Daisy instead of me? Maybe it's just a matter of time until he meets Daisy and realizes he could. But he's here with me.

The seagulls are swooping overhead, squawking cacophonously. I ask him what his real life looks like, and he tells me about his family in New Zealand, his parents who he thinks are great and his sister who's an architect and who he describes as the smartest person he knows.

'What about you? Do you get on with your parents?'

I pause for a second before answering. 'I don't really have a dad. But my mum is the best in every way, so I don't really notice it.'

He nods, thoughtfully. 'Did you ever have a dad?'

'Nope. I mean, obviously at some point eighteen years ago I did, but he opted out of the whole . . . scenario,' I say, gesturing in the air in an attempt to encompass the general concepts of responsibility and fatherhood. 'I've never met him and I don't need to. My mum met him when she was travelling before going to university to become a vet. And that's what she did, even though she had two tiny babies to look after.'

'Wow . . . your mum sounds amazing. But also – two?'

'I have a sister, too. Except she's my *twin* sister.'

'That's really cool!' Cal says, and sounds like he means it. 'I bet she's not as pretty as you, though,' he continues, which makes me want to laugh out loud. I manage to suppress that instinct.

'Oh, I assure you she is. I've spent my whole life being made *very* aware that Daisy is the pretty twin and I'm the dud. But it's OK, I'm at peace with it,' I say, dusting my hands off on my lap so I can press my hands together in mock prayer and close my eyes.

'Hey . . .' Cal says, putting his hand on my arm. I open my eyes and see that he looks genuinely pained. 'I don't love you talking like that about yourself . . .'

'I was mostly joking,' I say, even though I actually wasn't. It doesn't matter how good I am, how good I feel on my own, the world wants me to know that I can't compete when I'm standing next to Daisy.

Cal moves his hand to my face and tucks a lock of hair behind my ear. The setting sun is glinting off his bright blue eyes, making them sparkle like the sea in front of us. He is, without a shadow of a doubt, very, very handsome indeed. And I am possessed by the strong feeling that this very, very handsome guy is about to kiss me.

'Is it cool if I . . .' Cal begins.

'Yeah,' I say, nodding. So he kisses me. And it

obliterates every drunken party snog, every pointless crush, and every disappointing and underwhelming kiss I've ever had. It's so good that I don't know how to believe it's real.

As we're walking back from the pier towards the high street, a guy crosses our path. He looks kind of dishevelled, possibly homeless, and is carrying a big backpack.

'Alright, Cal!' he says, to my great surprise.

'Alright, Steve!' Cal replies brightly before the man keeps walking.

'Friend of yours?' I ask.

'Yeah, sort of . . .' he replies, shiftily. 'When it's quiet at work and my manager isn't around I let homeless people sit in the foyer. A few people sleep behind the cinema anyway, so what's the difference to me whether they're inside or outside, right? I mean, other than that I can do something to make their day a bit less shitty.'

'Oh . . .' I say, smiling. 'That's really nice, actually.' I'm embarrassed of the drily ironic tone I used when I asked if the guy was his friend. Cal's a better person than I am.

'I try to make myself useful where I can, you know?' he says casually.

'How come you chose the cinema?'

'Well, it was partly because they were advertising the

job and I needed money, but also because I genuinely love films.'

'What films?' I ask.

'I know it sounds weird but I'm really not that fussy – I'll watch anything.'

'Anything?' I repeat, incredulous.

'Yeah . . . old MGM musicals, blockbusters that are just released, blaxploitation films, noirs, romcoms – I'm easy!' Cal says, cheerily. 'Oh, the only thing I don't like is realistic violence or gore.' He shudders at the very thought.

'So you could watch a giant crocodile chomp a guy in half but you couldn't watch . . . say . . .' I cast about, trying to think of an example.

'You know the Tom Hanks film *Castaway*, right?'

'Oh sure, you mean the bit where he has to take his own tooth out?' I turn my nose up.

'Not even! I always think of that bit where he cuts his foot on a rock! I feel like that gives you a good indication of my tolerance for gore,' he says, grimacing.

'Wow!' I laugh. 'It's not like it's a bad thing, though.' I'm thinking of the boys Daisy has gone out with who would literally rather die than admit to being scared or disgusted or horrified, or even admit that they feel anything at all.

'I guess not.' He smiles. A very, very good smile.

We keep strolling through the streets of the town, past

the little candy-coloured terraces around the seafront, down the high street with its array of shops that haven't been done up in years and past the old-fashioned ice-cream parlour (Palmer's Ices' biggest rival). The papered-over windows of the old Bonner's department store are staring at us like two blank eyes. The dead shop has become so much a part of the town's scenery that I had barely noticed it for years, but now it looms over us like an accusation. I shiver in the warm night.

'I wonder what this town was like in the good old days,' says Cal, catching me looking at the department store. It's only in that moment, seeing Weston Bay through his eyes, that I realize quite how much it's changed. It's like it's all happened without me noticing. I suppose it's been happening for years. One shop closing down, then another; sometimes something appears in their place, sometimes it doesn't. It's a slow process. 'Probably wouldn't have been half as cute without you, though,' he adds, slipping his hand into mine as we walk.

Finally we stop, ready to part ways, except we're clearly not ready at all. Cal drops my hand and holds me by my waist, looking at me at arm's length. I let out a nervous giggle. But I feel emboldened, somehow, and I tip up onto my toes and kiss him hard on the mouth like I'll never get the chance to again. Like I'm in control of my life. Like

I'm happening to life, not life happening to me. It's play-acting, but it works. My hand on his shoulder, his holding my face, I realize we are in the positions of the lovers in Francesco Hayez's beautiful painting 'The Kiss', something I've looked at over and over, trying to absorb the passion and the urgency.

As I'm walking home, I finally, truly, believe that I have to tell Daisy about Cal. It's just a question of when. And how.

# CHAPTER FIVE

Molly? From your old school?

That's a weird person to be having breakfast with.

I mean, she's right, but also . . . I'm kind of looking forward to seeing someone I'm not so close to. I feel like everyone knows me better than I know myself at the moment.

Yeah . . . she's not so bad.
Except she's running late,
which is a thing I forgot people do.

The audacity?! I would never! At least today's new thing can be hanging out with someone who isn't me!!!

Before I can reply, she texts again.

I'm seeing Jack later 👀

I feel like she's expecting me to say something about Cal in return, but I don't. I'm not sure why.

Finally, Molly appears, her blonde curls bouncing as she sits down in front of me.

'Oh my god, how are you?! It's been ages!' No apology for being late. This is fine, apparently.

'I'm . . . doing OK, I think?'

'Amazing!'

'How about you?'

'Yeah, I'm good!' Molly nods eagerly, enunciating the words emphatically, like she's learned this way of speaking from a TV presenter. 'Do you know what you want?' She cranes her neck to attract the attention of the waitress.

'Uh, yeah, I think so . . .'

The waitress comes over, fishing in the pocket of her gingham pinafore for her notepad and pencil.

'What can I get for you?'

'Can I please have the blueberry pancakes and an orange juice?' I ask, folding the menu and handing it to her. 'Thanks so much.'

'Excellent choice.' She smiles as she notes it down. 'We squeeze our orange juice fresh.'

'I know you do! It's wonderful.'

'And how about for you?' she asks Molly.

'One poached egg on one slice of toast and a black

coffee,' Molly says, barely looking up from her phone.

'Alright . . .' says the waitress, as I give her an apologetic smile.

'Brown bread,' Molly adds, flatly.

'Thanks again!' I say, brightly, and the waitress gives me a sympathetic smile in return.

'You must be hungry,' Molly says as she slides her phone into her pocket. 'The blueberry pancakes here are *massive*.'

I feel myself blush at the implicit judgement of my choice, and I suddenly remember how uncomfortable Molly always made me feel about my body, even when we were friends. 'Yeah, I had a big night,' I reply, wondering if that will provoke further questioning on the subject. It doesn't.

'When did we last see each other? I was trying to remember on the way here.'

'I guess it was maybe last summer? I bumped into you on AS results night, right?' I say, trying to cast my mind back.

'Oh yeah! At Josh Patton's party!' Ugh. That party. I'd let Daisy drag me along because she really fancied Josh, and it paid off because they were together for a few months after that. Cassie said she didn't want to go so went drinking on the beach with some people from college instead, and I later found out it was because one of Josh's friends had forced her to kiss him at a party earlier that year. Obviously I did not enjoy myself and spent the whole time wishing I was drinking cans on the beach with Cassie.

'What are you up to these days? Are you doing the whole university thing or have you got a job already?' I ask as the waitress sets our drinks down on the table.

'I'm taking a gap year,' Molly says, blowing on her coffee. 'Going travelling. I want to see the world, you know, before I get stuck in the whole cycle of uni and work and everything.'

'Oh, cool! Where are you going?'

'Well, I really want to do South America. I want to go to Mexico and Costa Rica . . .' I let her go on without mentioning that neither Mexico nor Costa Rica are in South America. 'And I want to do Colombia, Brazil and Argentina,' she says, before taking a sip of her coffee. There is something about her use of the word 'do' that strikes me as arrogantly colonial, as if all of these amazing places are just items on a list to be ticked off and somehow conquered by her. Maybe that's how she approaches everything.

'That sounds amazing,' I reply diplomatically. 'I guess it's going to be a big trip . . . are you working at the moment to save for it?'

'Oh, no.' She shakes her head. 'My parents said it wouldn't be right for me to go to uni without having some adventure first.'

'OK . . .' I say, not really getting her meaning.

'So, they're paying.' She shrugs, as if that's extremely normal.

'Right . . . wow, OK,' I say with a nod, as our food arrives. I wonder if my mum would pay for me and Daisy to have a jolly for several months, even if she could. Probably not. She's too sensible.

'Ugh, those pancakes look *amazing*,' Molly says enviously. 'But I want to get really skinny for travelling.'

I'm about to tell her that she already *is* really skinny, but I know that's what she wants me to say, so I just eat my pancakes in peace while wishing I was back at home eating breakfast with Mum or on the big, squishy leather sofa at Cassie's house eating Pop-Tarts and watching cooking programmes while her parents go over the week's accounts for the shop. I don't care much whether Molly means to be fat-shaming me or not, but I *want* my life to be populated with people who see things the way I do: people who see beyond bodies. I don't want to have to listen to this from anyone.

'So . . . do you see much of anyone from school? Any excitement I've missed?' I ask. Seems like fairly neutral conversational territory to distract us from her casual campaign against my body.

After swallowing down a mouthful of her one poached egg on one slice of toast, Molly takes a deep breath before her features arrange themselves in a smug smile. 'OK, so where do I start with all the news! Did you hear about Georgia?'

'Georgia Reid?' I'm instantly concerned – Georgia was always a bit of a magnet for mess and disaster. You know, getting a bit too drunk at parties, being a bit too loud in class. Most famously, she once had to get rescued by the lifeboat when the tide came in and she was out for a walk, which is the *one thing* you're taught to be wary of when you grow up by the sea. But she was always kind to everyone at school.

'Yeah, Georgia Reid,' Molly replies, taking a sip of her coffee. I can tell she's loving this, whatever it is.

'No, what's happened to her?'

'Apparently she's "bi" now,' Molly says, waggling her fingers exaggeratedly either side of her head.

'What's with the air quotes?' I ask, my tone prickly.

Molly frowns at me, a look of infinite superiority on her smug face. 'Come on,' she begins, a look of cartoonish skepticism on her face. 'She was always a bit of an attention seeker, wasn't she?'

I have to pick my battles, and decide to overlook Molly's classification of Georgia's previous escapades as attention-seeking. But there are some battles I want to fight. Like those of an absent person who can't defend themselves.

'Can you elaborate on how her being bi' – I feel my face grow warm – 'works in this "attention-seeking" narrative?'

'It's just a cool thing to do now, isn't it? It doesn't even *mean* anything! It's just what people say when they're *desperately* trying to seem more interesting.'

I squint at her like I don't understand. 'It means she's bi. That's what it means.'

She widens her eyes at me. 'Alright, alright . . . it's not a huge thing, I just wanted to update you on the St Josephine's news.'

I don't want to talk about it anymore. Talking about Georgia behind her back is bad enough, but knowing that this is how Molly feels is even worse. I wonder if this is what everyone thinks.

We make conversation over the rest of our breakfast, largely about Molly rather than me, but my heart isn't really in it. I did try, though! I come away from the whole encounter feeling very secure in my decision to only hang out with Cassie. I had tried to remember the good things about Molly but in the process had managed to forget all the reasons I wasn't keen to stay in touch with her in the first place. And that includes not hanging out with people who make me feel uncomfortable. There are so many things in life that I can't control, so I might as well control the things that I can.

*

On the way back from breakfast, I decide to swing past Daisy's football game with her informal gang of sporty girls who play five-a-side (or however-many-a-side depending how many of them turn up) on the playing field every Sunday morning, indiscriminate of season. I figure we can walk home together and I can shake off my bad Molly vibes. As I approach the park, two middle-aged men pass me on the pavement. 'Bunch of dykes,' one says to the other, nodding towards Daisy and her friends.

'They're not bad-looking birds,' the other man replies, shaking his head. 'What a waste.'

I stop dead in my tracks as they keep walking in the opposite direction. I feel a white-hot fury rise in my body. It's anger as well as confusion – firstly the assumption that they must be gay because they're playing football, secondly that it's fine to use a slur against them even if they are, thirdly that they're just out here, roaming the streets looking at every woman they come across through the lens of whether or not they find them sexually appealing, and finally, that they're disgusting old men turning that lens on literal teenagers. I want to chase after them and beat them up, or at least yell at them. But I don't. Instead I just stand there for a second, feeling my palms get slick with sweat and listening to my breathing deepen. I don't want to share a world, let alone a town, with those men.

I want to unload my outrage on Daisy but there's no point, they're long gone. I just wait for her to say her goodbyes and bounce sweatily over to me.

'Fun?' I ask her as we head in the direction of home.

'Really fun! Too hot though,' she says, before taking a swig from her water bottle. 'I wasn't expecting to be escorted home!' She nudges me playfully with her hip as we walk.

'Yeah . . . I just wanted to get back to Planet Earth as soon as possible . . .'

'So Molly was . . .'

'Exactly as I should have known she would be.'

'Damn.'

I take a moment to arrange my thoughts. I steel myself. 'So . . . there was something I wanted to talk to you about.'

'Oh yeah?'

'Uh . . . about, like, dating, I guess . . .'

'Oh my god! Little Lily is all grown up! Tell me your troubles, I can advise you,' Daisy crows, triumphantly. I hate it.

'Ugh, I don't need *advice*!' I bite back, feeling my pulse quicken and years of resentment bubbling up beneath the surface.

'Alright!' Daisy says incredulously, like she can't imagine

why I would find her reaction annoying. 'Chill out!' Has anyone who's ever been told to chill out managed to chill out rather than become increasingly furious?

'It's fine. Whatever,' I say, quickening my pace to walk ahead of her.

She jogs to catch up with me. 'Ha, as if you could ever outrun me!' Because of course a little dig at how unathletic I am is what I need to feel like opening up to her. 'So?'

'Ugh, why do you even have to bring that up?'

'What?'

'All I wanted was to talk to you about some personal stuff and you still have to drop in some little comment about how much better you are than me.'

'That's not—' Daisy falters. 'I didn't! Look, just talk to me?'

'No. It's fine. I'm not bothered.' She knows to drop it. My irritation subsides bit by bit on the walk home, but it doesn't change the fact I still haven't told her about Cal.

I'm grateful to spend the afternoon on the sofa with Mum and Daisy watching endless reruns of *Come Dine with Me*. It's exactly the kind of normal I need right now.

'So . . .' Mum asks when Daisy's gone to make us cups of tea. 'How was the date?'

I can't help smiling, but know I can't talk about this too much with Daisy around. I guess Mum knows it's something

I don't want broadcast, otherwise she wouldn't have waited until now to ask. 'It was good.'

'That's all you want to tell me?' Mum raises her eyebrows expectantly.

'For now, yes.'

'Hmm.' Mum turns back to the TV. 'I don't like it but I accept it.'

In no time at all it's Sunday evening and we're at Gran's, reprising an old tradition that we've let slip for the past few weeks. Sunday night dinner, with me, Daisy, our mum, our Uncle Michael, his husband Mark and my gran. We used to rotate the hosting duties, but our dining table is really too small to fit six people around;, we figured Michael and Mark probably deserve a break from being the perfect hosts at the pub;, and besides, everyone just wants Gran's Yorkshire puddings anyway. Who wouldn't. They're perfect.

And I guess Gran is sort of perfect, too. We spent so much time around here when we were little, before we could take care of ourselves after school, when Mum was still at work. Gran only worked part-time then, doing the mornings at the visitor information centre near the castle on the edge of town. She would pick us up from school and walk us round to her house and watch children's TV and game shows with us give us Garibaldi biscuits and let Daisy help her in the garden. When I look at it now, I realize how small it is, but Gran takes such good care of it and makes the most of the space she has, so it used to feel like acres. That's what made Daisy love gardening so much. Whereas I showed no interest and was allowed to stay inside with colouring pencils and a pile of paper. That's what's so good about Gran. She just let us be who we were and helped us become those people without forcing it. I know teenagers are meant to crave independence but, in a way, I missed my afternoons at Gran's when it was decided we could walk home on our own and look after ourselves for the couple of hours between school finishing and Mum coming home from the vet's. Back then, Uncle Michael was running a pub in London, which is where he met Mark, and they only moved here a few years ago, so for a long time it was just me and Daisy and Mum and Gran.

When we arrive at Gran's it's hugs all round before piling into the small, cosy living room overflowing with pot plants and china. My mum and Uncle Michael start laying the table while Gran pulls trays with steaming, crispy, golden roast potatoes out of the oven. Mark asks me and Daisy questions about what we're up to this summer ('not a lot') and we make him tell us about all the badly-behaved patrons of the Lighthouse until it's time to eat. He refuses to name names, but we know that at least one of our old teachers is on his shit list and we're going to make it our life's work to find out who.

We crowd around the big dining table that takes up almost half the room and start eating the perfect roast beef and those roast potatoes I saw emerging from the oven, cooked in goose fat and semolina.

A few seconds later, Uncle Michael leaps up. 'Oh, I don't want to forget!' He dashes from the room and returns with two copies of the same book. 'For you two, so you don't starve.' He hands a copy to each of us. *100 Recipes For Hungry Students.*

'Thanks so much,' I say as enthusiastically as I can manage. Not that I'm not grateful for the book. It just feels like all around me are reminders that I really am going. I really am leaving. That's what's happening. I really am being given the autonomy and the independence I thought I should be craving.

If I look flustered, no one notices, because Daisy is delighted at the chance to talk about how she'll be studying physics at Bristol Uni. 'As long as I get the grades!' she always adds, as if there's any doubt. Much like the football and the gardening, I don't exactly understand what Daisy sees in physics, or even in science in general, but I'm happy for her that she seems to have found her calling.

'Still can't believe you backed out of your twin dream plan, Lily!' Uncle Michael says good-naturedly, between mouthfuls of potato. 'It's going to be such an adventure for you!'

A tension descends on Daisy and me. A Daisy's-prickling-with-irritation-at-my-uni-choice-flavoured tension. I realize no one's saying anything, so I fill the silence. 'It won't be so bad . . . not so different from now . . .' I venture. 'We're not at college together or anything.'

'Well, I mean we probably won't see each other much, will we?' Daisy asks me. I'm a little taken aback by the question. I guess because I'm using a lot of brain energy on trying not to think about the fact I'm going away from everything. And Daisy is so carefree and independent, I'm surprised she's even thinking about it at all.

'I guess not,' I say. 'Leeds and Bristol are quite far apart.'

'Yeah, and I guess I'll come home to see everyone. Maybe we can time some visits so we're in sync?'

'Maybe, yeah,' I say, non-committally. I feel like if I even think about going home in term time, I'll want to go home every weekend. And I can't do that. I mean, for starters, I probably wouldn't even be able to afford the train fare. I certainly won't be having dinner with my lovely family every Sunday night. I thought I was so ready for a big adventure, but really all I want is this.

Daisy gives me a strange look and Mark mercifully chooses that moment to change the topic.

'You're going to have a lot of time on your hands at the end of the summer, aren't you, Lucy?' he asks Mum, pouring gravy on his plate.

Uncle Michael pipes up, 'Maybe now's the time to think about . . .' He wiggles his eyebrows. 'A boyfriend?'

Mum rolls her eyes as if that's the most ludicrous thing she's ever heard from her brother.

'Come on, Luce! I know you've got loads going on with work and looking after the girls, but now . . .' Michael shrugs and raises his hands in a gesture of open contemplation. He's right. We're pretty much all grown up, and I know that Daisy and I are uncharacteristically united in our desire to see our mum happy. Her time can be her own again for the first time in years.

'Alright, alright . . . it's not like I'm *not* thinking about it,' she concedes.

'Well there we are!' my uncle says triumphantly.

'Jade's got me on the apps. All of them. I'm not used to getting this many notifications, it's stressing me out a bit . . .' At that, Mum slips her phone out of her pocket and looks at it with an expression of fear before putting it back again, out of sight.

'Tell me one more time: what's an app?' Gran asks.

Uncle Michael leans over and whispers an explanation to her. Gran frowns but seems to accept it.

'So, any luck?' Michael asks.

'Well . . .' Mum blushes and looks down at her plate.

'Oh my god!' Michael gasps with glee.

'It's not a big thing! Just one date. I want to try new things.' Mum glances at me and smiles.

'Yeah! No pressure, Lucy. I wish you the best of luck!' Mark says.

Mum furrows her brow and says, 'It's funny, you know, it seems like most men my age don't know how to take a photo of themselves.'

'What do you mean?' Gran asks.

'Somehow they all end up looking like thumbs?' Mum shakes her head, perplexed. 'Like they take a selfie from below in bad lighting and think that's enough to get them a date!'

'I don't think that's a men-your-age problem, I think that's a straight-men problem!' Mark quips.

'You're meeting him in a public place, being sensible and all that, right?' asks Uncle Michael, with the intensity of an only sibling.

'Bloody hell, Michael, I'm not going to meet him at his house or in a dodgy car park or anything!'

'Not on a first date anyway,' I mumble into my glass of lemonade.

'We're meeting at the Rat and Parrot if that makes you feel any better!'

'The Rat and Parrot?' Uncle Michael squints at her in sheer disbelief that those words could have come out of her

96

mouth. 'That's literally the most random choice of date venue I've ever heard – what is he, eighty years old?'

'It is a bit of a weird choice, Mum,' I agree. Every pub in Weston Bay has its own unique quality, and the Rat and Parrot's is that it's very much an old man pub. A *very* old man pub. If you can call that a unique quality. It's dark and poky, smells a little damp, is nowhere near the town centre and is, as you can probably guess, largely frequented by old men.

'Weird or not weird, that's what's happening, and I assure you I will be telling you no more about it if you're going to be like this!' Mum throws up her hands defensively.

'Well, I think it's great,' says Mark, smiling broadly. It's good to have a non-Rose in the mix. A moderating influence to stop us yelling excitedly at each other for hours. 'I hope your date goes well and the Rat and Parrot turns out to be surprisingly conducive to romance.' He tilts his wine glass in my mum's direction.

'Mark, how did you, a kind and gentle soul, end up married to someone as annoying as my little brother?'

'Sheer good luck,' Mark says, smiling at Uncle Michael as if he's the best thing in the world. They're the most normal couple I know. Well, they're one of the only couples I know. But they make it look like good fun. They're always laughing together, like they're in their own little world, and seem to make the perfect team in managing the pub together. I'd like something that easy. That assured. Maybe that's what Cal will be for me? At least for this summer, even if it won't be forever?

We polish off our roast and somehow still find room for Gran's sticky toffee pudding, which is absurd but no one can resist. We all leave there feeling full and warm and happy, and I hope my Gran feels that too, even though she's been left alone in her little house. But through that warm glow of family is a feeling that Daisy's definitely been a bit off with me since I chickened out of telling her about Cal.

# CHAPTER SIX

I'm on my usual route to work the next morning, clinging to the shaded side of the pavement like a limpet because it's already noticeably hotter than normal, when a poster catches my eye. It's stuck to the side of a derelict shop and shows a scene of Weston Bay from the Victorian era. Underneath it is a line of text saying, 'Don't you wish our town still looked like this? SAY NO TO MULTICULTURALISM IN WESTON BAY'. No indication of which group or party has put it up. The thought of it chills me and at the same time absolutely inflames me. I almost . . . can't believe it? It's scary that someone in this town would feel empowered to do it. I stand in front of the poster, wondering if I should take it down. I wish I had one of the cans of black spray-paint from the art room at college, but, weirdly, I don't take cans of spray paint to work with me. Also, I can't help but wonder if something worse would take the poster's place if I did tear it down. I can't let that hold me back. I just do it, tearing it off in strips from top to bottom until it's all gone. I ball up the paper and shove it into the nearest bin, which is already overflowing.

I reluctantly continue on to work, wondering how many other posters there are around town and what kind of person would put them up, and before long, I arrive at the ice-cream stand. Cassie is setting up the freezer and the generator just like her mum showed us on the first day we were open.

'Cool jumpsuit!' I say to Cassie while her head is stuck in the freezer compartment. I'm rubbing suntan lotion on my arms and face. Being freckly, I am very prone to burning, which is not a cute look.

'Thanks!' she replies, standing upright to greet me. 'I didn't make this one, sadly.'

'I bet you could, though.'

'All in good time.' I pass her the suntan lotion, which she grudgingly accepts even though she jokingly claims to 'literally' never burn, since she's half Jamaican. 'Hey, how was your weekend?'

'Yeah, it was fine. Seeing Molly reminded me why I only like hanging out with you.'

'Nothing else . . .? Nothing else to report?' Cassie asks with a slight air of confusion.

'Oh yeah!' I say, realizing what she's asking. I feel so distracted by the poster that I'm barely concentrating. 'I saw Cal, as you know. That was . . .' I blush and try to suppress a smile. 'Much better than hanging out with Molly.'

'After I *My-Fair-Lady*-ed you, Jack told me how nervous Cal was to go and meet you! I guess that means Cal is talking about you to him! That's a good sign!'

'Yeah, I guess so.' I say. 'So you saw Jack?'

'We went out last night, just to the cinema. It's weird, I thought he wouldn't want to, since he works there. But nope, that was his suggestion!'

'And how was it?' I ask, though for some reason I'm not sure I want to know.

Cassie blushes and looks down at the tubs she's putting into the freezer. 'Yeah. Good.'

'Nothing more than that?'

'It was nice, you know. It's weird, I feel like I went into the whole thing not really knowing what to expect, but I actually had a pretty good time.'

'What do you mean, not knowing what to expect?'

'I guess I wondered if he only asked me out because Cal asked you out and it made a nice symmetry or whatever.'

'Oh,' I say, genuinely surprised. 'I don't get why you would think that . . . of course he would want to ask you out? You're like . . . a thousand times too good for him?'

'I mean . . . maybe?'

'Are you kidding?!' I ask, incredulously.

'I'm not fishing for compliments here!' Cassie holds her

hands up defensively but can't help laughing.

'Well, all I'm saying is you're perfect.' I pause for a second. 'God, I hope my mum meets someone nice.'

'Oh?'

'Yeah, I've "inspired" her,' I tell Cassie. 'With my new things, you know? She's decided it's time to date.'

'After all this time . . .' Cassie sounds like she's in awe of my mum already.

'Yep.'

'Well, she's a babe. And a professional, adult woman. And you two are gonna be out of her hair soon. What's not to like?' I mean, *I* don't like the thought of being out of her hair, but I don't tell Cassie that.

For a very sunny day it's a weirdly slow morning, which we pass with endless rounds of 'would you rather?' at which Cassie is incredibly creative. A seagull's head on your body, or your head on a seagull's body? Tell our stuffy, middle-aged former art teacher you're desperately in love with him, or only drink seawater for a week? Cassie's also got a new time-wasting habit and has a little A6 notepad in which she sketches cute, stylized cartoons of people. Our customers make perfect material, because they all look so different from each other and you can never predict who'll come by next.

'Maybe it's because I'm incurably nosy,' begins Cassie, 'but I always want to know what people's stories are.'

'It's funny when you make yourself think about people like that . . .' I say. 'I guess it's easy to forget that everyone has the same kind of rich interior life that you do, and we only kind of . . . rub up against a tiny fraction of what that life is made up of.'

'I love it, what a thought. What a concept!' Cassie says, dropping the ice-cream scoop into the water tub to clean it and adjusting her baseball cap. 'I guess I just assume that whatever people show me is what they really are.' I wonder then how much of myself I'm ever really showing. And whether that's a good or a bad thing.

Last week was hot, but this week is a certifiable heatwave. The grass on the green that we trade from isn't so much green as a parched, straw-like beige, and the sea is shimmering invitingly. I can't think too much about how incredible the cool water would feel against my skin, how much I want to let the sweat-matted hair under my baseball cap mingle with the seawater.

By the afternoon there's a steady stream of customers. Honeycomb emerges as the must-have flavour of the day. My mum texts me to remind me she's out tonight, *But you and Daisy can feed yourselves, I'm quite sure of it!* I wish her luck on her date even though the thought of my mum going out to meet a man is a bit weird as well as nice.

'Doesn't that lilo look like a juicy ice lolly,' Cassie asks, nodding towards a pink lilo and foam noodle that a day tripper's abandoned on the beach.

'Don't eat the lilo,' I warn her. 'The heat's gone to your brain.'

'It's just a lot, isn't it?'

'It's definitely a lot,' I say, as a bead of sweat drips from my eyebrow onto my eyelashes and into my eyes.

While we're closing up for the day, I feel my phone vibrate in my pocket and I slip it out to see a text from Cal.

Hey! I thought I would have heard
from you by now, hope you're doing OK?

I'm a bit taken aback. Is this normal? I haven't really had an ongoing thing with a guy before . . . I'm still not sure of the rules of engagement – you know, whether to text first, how keen to be, how fast to move. See, this would be Daisy's area of expertise. She'd know the answer. But maybe those things aren't actually important. Maybe I should just do what I want. Do what I feel. Is it weird that, as much as I mega fancy him, I haven't really worried about texting him? I text him back, apologizing for not having been in touch and asking if he wants to do something tomorrow night, although the thought of doing anything in this heat other than flopping in the shade like a dog nearly makes me delete the message.

'It's hot, isn't it?' I say to Cassie lamely, putting my phone away. Of course it's hot. It's a heatwave.

'Yeah. It's too hot. I want to jump in the sea right this minute.'

'Me too. More than anything in the whole world, I think.'

Cassie looks at me out of the corner of her eye, like a thought is brewing inside her brain. 'You know . . . we could?'

I look at her with an expression of confusion. 'But we don't have any stuff with us? No swimsuits, no towels?'

'So what?! We can't let that stop us! We can go in in our underwear, no one will know the difference anyway? And in this heat, we'll dry off quick as you know it if we just lie on the beach for a bit,' she says eagerly.

'Covered in sand?'

'Obviously it'll look entirely bizarre, but we do have a whole roll of bin liners here which we could take to lie on.'

'Baking my salty body on a pile of binbags is not how I envisaged spending this evening, if I'm honest,' I say, stalling for time.

'Where's your sense of adventure?' Cassie pleads.

'You know sense of adventure is your domain.'

'Yes but also this is *low-risk* adventure.'

Through my uncertainty, I grin at Cassie, knowing what she's contrasting this with. 'You mean it's not like when you decided it was essential for us to take up skateboarding because you never saw any girls at the skate park in Hook Green?'

'I knew your wrist wasn't broken!'

'It was sprained though!'

'A skateboarding career cut short, is all I'm saying.'

'You could have gone back without me!'

'Yeah but it wouldn't have been fun without you, so . . .' She trails off, keeping her tone casual, but it pings a little glow inside me. 'Anyway, a quick post-work swim is today's new thing. I've just decided it. I make the rules around here.'

It's not like I haven't been swimming with Cassie before. It's just part of normal life when you live by the sea. But something's making me hold back, even though I want to feel that cool water against my skin more than anything. I would normally wear a swimsuit rather than a bikini, so the thought of being out there in bra and knickers makes me feel exposed. But then again, swimming in my underwear in broad daylight isn't a bad way to push myself out of my comfort zone, is it? And surely the town won't explode if people see my body as it really is? I nibble my lip and think about the divide between the life I'm living and the life I could be living.

Cassie squints at me. 'This isn't a body thing, is it?'

'No!' I protest.

'Because I can't imagine what reason you'd have for not wanting to come for a swim after a hard day's toil in this dumb temperature.'

'OK, fine, maybe I *am* feeling a bit weird at the moment . . . those guys heckling me and throwing stuff at me when I was jogging, and then, ugh, seeing Molly who just made me feel so . . . different from her, like I was an alien or something . . .' I flush with shame at actually voicing some vulnerability instead of keeping it all inside.

'We've been through this before, my dude,' Cassie says, patiently. 'You have *got* to stop letting other people's shitty opinions and behaviour affect the way you feel about yourself. You *know* you're cute. You *know* there's nothing wrong with your body. And then some random *loser* comes along and destabilizes your self-worth? Nuh-uh.' Cassie shakes her head definitively.

'But what if that's just . . . not true? I . . . like, really admire the way you don't think about your body at all. And I want that for myself, but it's hard, you know? It feels like no matter what I think, I still have to share a planet with people who are so *negative* about bodies that are different.' What I don't say is that sometimes those people are your own twin sister.

'It's hard, I get that! I was a scrawny, skinny little kid and now I am the . . . voluptuous giantess you see before you today!' Cassie says, throwing her arms wide like her soft, curvy body is the centre of the universe. 'It's not like I couldn't be that skinny little chicken if I tried. I just don't feel like I have to. And it didn't come out of nowhere for me – I don't think *anyone's* born with confidence – or if you are, it gets beaten out of you pretty quickly. You just have to, like, relentlessly do the work. Relentlessly believe in your right to look however you want to look. Or however you *do* look, whether you want to or not! Just standing firm.'

I let her words sink in. It sounds so good. It sounds like a place I want to live in permanently, not just visit. 'God . . . it's tough, isn't it?'

'It is! But you're tougher. We both are.' She rests her hands on my shoulders and looks me in the eyes. I want to look away but I force myself not to. 'As your best friend it is my responsibility, no, my *extreme joy* to remind you that you are the cutest in the whole world, and no amount of terrible men or boring girls can change that.'

'I guess . . .'

'I don't want you to feel pressured – you know I'm gonna go swimming whether you come or not, right?' Cassie shrugs, dropping her hands to her sides. I can still feel their warm pressure on my shoulders. 'I just want to have fun with you! Make the most of the time we have left this summer, right?'

This hits me right in the stomach. 'Oh, go on then,' I concede quickly.

'Excellent. You won't regret it. But first, we need sustenance for our aquatic adventure,' says Cassie. We stop at the seafood hut and buy little polystyrene cups of cockles, which we drench in vinegar and prepare to eat with the poky toothpicks, and my old friend the seafood man undercharges us.

'It's been a scorcher today, hasn't it?'

'You're telling us! If you ever want to take a break while our stand is up, come over and we'll do you a deal,' I say to him before we head for the sea.

'But not on weekends,' Cassie interjects quickly. 'I'd get in so much trouble if Graham grassed me up to my parents for giving people discounts.'

'You know he would.' I roll my eyes.

'That's very kind of you, girls. Ordinarily I wouldn't, but since it's Palmer's, I'll find that hard to resist!' The warmth I feel towards him is familiar – the complete opposite of the raw ball of fury I felt at that poster earlier today. This town has hope yet.

We wander off to sit on the sea wall and eat our cockles, feeling smug in the knowledge that we work at the finest ice-cream stand in Weston Bay.

Out of nowhere, Cassie grabs my arm. 'Mate!'

'What?!' I ask, trying not to topple off the wall.

Cassie's pointing wildly to the right of where we're sitting. 'The floats are still there! It's a sign! Come on . . .' She hops down and holds out a hand for me to hop down after her. I feel ridiculous and ungainly but I do it anyway.

'This is perfect! Perfect!' Cassie picks up the foam noodle and nudges the lilo towards me with her foot.

'I'll agree, it does seem like a sign,' I say, hoisting it under my arm.

We slide our shoes off and continue down towards the sea in our bare feet, first on the clattering, shifting pebbles, and then the sand, almost unbearably hot against the soles of our feet after baking under the blazing sun all day. When we reach the shore, we stand with our toes in the shallow water for a moment, basking in the tingling pleasure-pain of the cold, before Cassie turns to me and says, 'Ready?'

'Let's do it,' I say, and start pulling my T-shirt off over my head. I roll it into a sausage shape, slip off my culottes and roll them around the T-shirt before depositing both onto the sand, making sure my house keys and phone don't fall out, because, being me, I obviously can't fully switch off my impulse for caution even in spontaneous moments of fun. Cassie tears her clothes off, throwing her jumpsuit and the contents of her pockets down in a less orderly but far more indentifiably Cassie heap than mine, and we run, splashing and screaming, into the glittering sea, dragging our floats behind us.

Cassie bobs elegantly on her foam noodle while I do the hard physical labour of trying to get onto a lilo in the water. Finally I succeed and we rock harmoniously on the cool, blue water. We gossip about people from college, we talk about our plans for the future – the holidays we'll take together, the trips Cassie will take to Leeds when she can – we cackle and we shriek with delight.

'I'm coming in,' I say, shimmying off my purloined lilo. The cold of the water is thrilling again.

'I'm kind of done with this li'l guy, too,' says Cassie. 'Bless you, noodle, you served me well.'

'Let's put them back on the sand for someone else to nick.'

'Circle of life,' says Cassie as we trudge, dripping, out of the sea. I hope this doesn't mean we're done. For all I was resistant to the idea, now that I'm here I'm loving the feeling of the water and the sun on my skin and the fact that

I'm spending proper time with Cassie. 'Hey, you can go if you want, but I'm going to go back in,' she says.

'I have nowhere else to be,' I say, and we walk arm in arm back into the sea.

We swim out a little in a very unathletic breaststroke, keeping our heads above the water but splashing the sparkling, cool ocean on our faces. It feels like pure heaven to be there with my best friend, bobbing in the sea, with the sun low in the sky. No responsibilities. We float on our backs like starfish, closing our eyes and letting the salt water keep us afloat. I open one eye against the glare of the sun and think about how fun it would be to paint the sky from this perspective, a whole canvas of sky. Maybe that can be my next project.

Letting the waves rock me gently, my body supported by the water, I revel in the fact that I don't feel any animosity towards it. My body never lets me down. It does everything I need it to do. And with Cassie on my team, I feel like I can take on all of the rubbish that other people project onto me. All their assumptions and expectations. It strikes me that even when we were close, I never dreamed of doing this with Molly. It makes me wish everybody had a Cassie. Someone they can be completely themselves with, someone who brings out the best in them and helps them manage their insecurities.

As we float, our hands brush against each other and the jolt of surprise it gives me makes me stand up. I head out a bit further so I have a good excuse to pretend I haven't heard Cassie when she calls to me, 'Are you alright, Lily?'

When she repeats herself, I shout, 'What was that?'

'Actually, nothing, it's alright,' she replies. She doggy-paddles over to me. 'This is the good shit, isn't it? Aren't I a genius for suggesting it?'

'You are indeed a genius. This is just what I needed. Thank you.' We're bobbing in the water a little way out from the shore, where we can only just about stand up, our heads emerging from the surface of the sea.

Without saying anything, she puts her arms around me. She rests her head on my shoulder and wraps me up in a hug and I just stand there, a lump in my throat.

'I'll miss you,' she says finally. I feel a tear slide down my damp cheek. When she pulls away, I submerge myself in the water and open my eyes, reappearing only to complain about the stinging.

We splash around in the water before returning to the sand in the fading light, weirdly exhausted after having done little more than float and bob. We lie, ridiculously, on our black bin liners until we've dried off enough to put our clothes back on, beating the sand out of them before we can wear them. We sit on the beach and chat long enough to see the sun go down. My chest feels heavy but I don't know how to express the reasons why, and if I did I don't know that I would want to.

# CHAPTER SEVEN

New things I have done so far this week:

1. Watched a film in Korean. Cal's recommendation, but felt extremely cultured.
2. Nicked Daisy's liquid eyeliner and attempted my first-ever elegant cat-eye. Instead ended up with very avant-garde black horns on each eye. Maybe next time.
3. Made a whole lasagne *including my own béchamel sauce*. Not bad. OK, so Daisy *did* help me with that one but I'm still going to own it.
4. Cassie's big suggestion: went shopping for uni stuff. It made me feel a bit sick. But I bought a new duvet cover to show I'm committed.

Ever since our little swimming expedition earlier in the week, it's felt as if we're quieter than usual, although I can't exactly put my finger on why. A thin layer of awkwardness, of distance, has worked its way into our friendship. But today that distance feels oddly peaceful rather than tense or confrontational. Maybe peace and distance are what I need right now. We have an unusually busy morning which keeps us distracted, serving a steady stream of customers. A quiet moment gives Cassie a chance to dash to the pub nearby that lets us use their toilet, since we're kind of out here on our own.

I bend down to check we have enough napkins in the cupboard under the stand, and when I emerge Cal is standing right in front of me, as if he's appeared from a puff of smoke. He's wearing a polo shirt and trousers which I realize is his work uniform. No Daisy-at-the-garden-centre vibes here – he still manages to look like he picked it out himself this morning.

'I thought I might find you here.' He smiles. It's such a good smile it almost takes my breath away. I'm caught by surprise. Not just that he's there, but also by how much I'm drawn to him – he's gorgeous. He's genuine. He's . . . nice.

'Oh!' I say. Seeing him tonight and seeing him right now with zero warning or preparation are two very different things. And in this uncontrolled environment, there's nothing to stop Daisy from coming by for an ice cream and wanting to know why I'm chatting casually to the guy I know very well is her current target. 'Hi!'

'All alone?'

'Cassie's gone to use the toilet at the pub, so yeah, all on my own right now! Did you want some ice cream?'

'Yeah, why not,' he says with a shrug. 'I mostly just came by to see you, but who can resist ice cream in this weather?'

I blush. The thought of a guy like Cal going out of his way to see me at work is most certainly out of my comfort zone.

'What's your flavour?' I ask.

He peruses the flavours on offer under the glass case with great seriousness. 'Blood-orange sorbet,' he finally decides.

I prepare two perfect scoops in a cone and hand it over to him.

'Are you allowed to step round the wrong side of your stand?' Cal asks.

'Uhhh . . . I guess?' I reply, not really understanding.

'Otherwise I'll come round there,' he says.

'OK?'

He steps round the side of the stand, holding his ice cream off to one side with one hand and placing the other around my waist. He pulls me in close and kisses me, the peak of my stupid baseball cap knocking against his forehead. In one movement he smoothly lifts it off my head and pushes a fallen lock of hair behind my ear, seemingly undisturbed by the fact my hair is all matted and sweaty.

'Ohhh, so this is what you get up to when I go to the

loo!' Cassie's back, and, instinctively, I take a step back from Cal.

'Not every time, I assure you,' I say, rolling my eyes and ignoring whatever strange feeling is going on in my stomach.

'Hi, Cal,' she says.

'Hi, Cassie, nice to see you again. I just dropped by to pick up a cone on the way to work. It may only be a short shift today but I still need my fuel, right?'

'Right you are,' says Cassie, as Cal makes a start on his ice cream. He really makes eating a blood-orange sorbet look good. 'Hey, aren't you two going out tonight?'

'Yeah, we are, but I couldn't wait that long,' he replies. I smile, even though I'm more than a little confused about how someone can just be so straightforward. It's like he knows what he wants and he doesn't play games and just makes it clear what he's doing. I guess I can't really relate to being so sure of anything.

'Cute,' Cassie says, coming back round to our side of the stand.

'Well, I've paid my flying visit. I'd better hit the road. See what chaos your boy Jack's been wreaking with the matinees,' Cal says, winking at Cassie. He gives me a quick kiss before leaving.

It's only when Cal's disappeared into the distance that

I notice Cassie seems distracted, nibbling on her nails. 'What's up?' I ask her. 'Are you alright?'

She takes her fingers out of her mouth and runs the nails against her thumb. 'I broke a nail while I was away.'

'God, I thought you were going to tell me it was something serious like a paper cut.' I laugh. But Cassie doesn't smile.

'Yeah . . .' Cassie begins, and I can tell there's more to it than that, and she's turning over in her brain whether it's worth sharing the rest.

'OK . . . You can tell me, you know,' I reassure her. Even though it's irrational, I'm struck with the paranoid thought that it's something I've done.

After a pause, Cassie explains. 'I was tearing down a poster. One of those fascist ones. I couldn't walk past it again, so I just tore it down and ripped it up and shoved it in someone's wheelie bin.'

'That's amazing!'

'I don't think anyone saw me, but I'm worried I could get in trouble.'

'I don't think tearing posters down is a crime. Surely putting them up in the first place counts as vandalism . . .'

'I know, but you know how it is, they can always find an excuse . . .'

'Look, if anyone tries anything, there are about twenty

people I can think of off the top of my head who have your back. I'll say it was me. You did something good and useful and I'm sorry you had to,' I say, almost guiltily. I guess I do feel guilty. I should've done something to make sure Cassie didn't have to see one of those disgusting posters. They shouldn't be up at all. Wow. Guilt is featuring pretty heavily in my life right now.

'Thanks,' she says.

I think for a moment. 'If I see any, I'll take them down myself, so you don't have to worry about it anymore.'

'That'd be cool. Thank you,' Cassie says, nodding. 'Hey, it was nice of Cal to come by, right?'

'Yeah, I guess so . . .'

'You don't sound so sure?' Cassie presses me. I'm about to tell her about the whole Daisy situation, but I stop myself. I figure I should probably work it out with Daisy first, before telling Cassie. I can't keep it a secret for much longer, and I don't want to burden Cassie with a secret to keep too – she and Daisy actually get on pretty well.

'No, it's not that . . . it's just very new to me and I'm not sure how to handle it. That level of attention or interest or whatever.'

'It's a good thing. Don't worry about it too much.' Her attention is caught by a huge seagull swooping down and hopping about in front of the stand. 'GO AWAY! You can fly!' Cassie yells at it. 'I know we're hot babes but surely you have better places to be!'

The seagull does what it's told and flies off with a squawk. Cassie's quiet for a while, scratching away at her notebook, then holds it up and shows me a perfect little rendering of Cal: his thick, dark hair, his heavy eyebrows, his high cheekbones, and what you can tell, even in soft grey pencil, are his pale blue eyes.

'You're amazing,' I say to her.

A woman with two children approaches the stand. She's wearing a headscarf and a long-sleeved T-shirt and jeans, and the kids are running gleefully towards us. They're very excited about the prospect of ice cream but have no idea what flavour they want, so Cassie scrapes a little of each with a variety of our tiny transparent plastic spoons. Eventually they're able to place their perfect order and they wander off back to the seafront with their cones.

I don't say it out loud, but the idea that someone thinks our town would be better off without Cassie or this woman and her children makes me so confused and angry. I watch as Cassie pulls out her notebook and starts scribbling away. Weston Bay would be so empty without her. She belongs here. If she wasn't here . . . nothing would make sense.

It doesn't take long for Cassie to turn the family into a sweet little cartoon trio in her notebook. I don't know how she does it, they look so much like them, the little boy's smile, the folds in the woman's scarf. It makes me wonder if she's ever drawn me.

'You're really on a roll today, dude,' I say to her as she tucks her notebook into her back pocket.

'The infinite mystery of the human face. Hey, why don't you draw a nice portrait later as your new thing?' Cassie looks optimistic.

'I'll think about it . . .' I say evasively. I can tell she doesn't believe me.

Another honest day's work successfully behind me, I look at myself in my bedroom mirror. I definitely look a thousand times better than I did when Cal came by the stand earlier, so at least I've got that going for me. No more sweaty baseball-cap hair for Lily Rose. As I'm admiring myself, tucking my T-shirt into the tiger-print midi skirt Cassie made me for my birthday last year, my sister pops her head round the door.

'Can I borrow that pink lipstick you were wearing the other night?' Daisy asks. 'Oh, are you going out too? Maybe we can walk into town together.'

'Yeah, I'm just meeting –' I begin, without having figured out whose name I'm going to say. Probably Cassie's.

'Let me guess . . .' she says, and for a minute I'm sure she's going to say Cal. And although I know that if she does, and I wasn't the one to tell her, that I've crossed some kind of twin line, part of me would be so relieved for this to be all over and done with. 'Cassie?' I need to tell her. She needs to know.

But I'm a coward, and instead of coming clean I laugh nervously and rummage around on top of my chest of drawers, without actually answering the question. 'Here's the lipstick.'

She manages to apply it expertly without looking in the mirror. Predictably, it looks better on her.

'I'm ready,' she says triumphantly, as she clicks the cap back on and slips it into her pocket like it was hers all along.

'Where are you off to?' I ask, praying she says the Lighthouse. I realize I'm counting the beats of the syllables against the palm of my hand again. Where-are-you-off-to. I wiggle my fingers to force myself to stop. As if forcing myself to stop doing the thing I do when I feel tense and anxious is the same thing as actually stopping myself from feeling tense and anxious.

'Cinema with Charisse and Sabrina,' she says. 'Followed by the Lighthouse, just for a couple of drinks. I know Mark will make us some free cocktails while Uncle Michael isn't looking.' Bingo. No chance our paths will cross there. Looks like everything is coming up Lily.

'What are you seeing at the cinema?'

'Some stupid-looking romcom.' She shrugs. 'I'm mostly going because they want to see it.'

'Well, I hope it doesn't suck too hard.'

'And I'm thinking of giving my cinema crush my number,' she says, casually. 'You know, if he's there.'

*He won't be*, I think to myself. I've got to tell her. 'Maybe . . . he's already seeing someone?' I suggest, struggling to stay nonchalant.

'Ha!' Daisy replies absently, as she tosses her hair and pouts in the mirror. 'I'm sure she'll be no match for me either way.'

Something about this simple statement pierces me right through the heart. It's like, without knowing a thing, she has still managed to drill down deep into the core of all my fears.

I realize I haven't said anything after a few seconds. 'I wish you luck,' I say, finally. I slip on my shoes, pick up my bag and we head downstairs to say bye to Mum.

'Like ships in the night,' Mum says, shaking her head mock-forlornly. She's watching a cooking programme on TV. They're making some kind of elaborate chocolate torte. 'Last night I was out and you were home, tonight I'm home alone while my girls are out and about. Oh well, just a little taste of my future, I should probably get used to it.'

'Poor old Mummy,' I say, joining her on the sofa and

wrapping my arms around her. 'You won't be too bored without us, will you? You could always look for someone on the apps now and meet them in an hour.'

'No, of course I won't be bored!' Mum scoffs. 'And what would you do if I said yes, eh? Are you going to stay home and hang out with me rather than going on a d—'

'Mum!' I interject.

'Hmm?' Daisy asks, looking up from her phone, as if the only reason she tuned in was because she could detect my tone, but hadn't actually heard anything.

'Nothing,' I say, casually. 'Hey, he's cute.' I point at the screen, where a red-headed chef with thick-rimmed glasses is piping icing onto the torte.

'He *is* cute,' says Mum.

'I'm not into gingers. And besides, I could never date a chef, I'd get so fat,' Daisy says. Before I can even figure out how to react, let alone actually do it, Daisy turns to Mum. 'Hey, are you going to see your internet man again?'

Mum can't suppress her smile, but pauses before replying. 'Yes, I hope so . . .'

'Wow! Can't believe you got a good one on the first go!' Daisy says in disbelief.

'It was a good first date, that's all.' Mum shrugs, but the smile is still there. 'He doesn't live in town but has to come for work pretty much every week.'

'So he stays in a . . . hotel?' I say, wiggling my eyebrows.

'Ugh, gross!' Daisy's having none of it. 'Hey, what's this?' She nudges a big box on the floor with her foot.

'Woks!' Mum cries, delightedly.

'Rocks?' Daisy peers at her, uncomprehending. 'A box of rocks?'

'W-o-k, wok. A truly indispensable item for any student, I assure you.'

'Argh, I feel like everyone buying me stuff for next year is jinxing it! What if I don't get the grades and I have to sit around here for another year with this wok staring at me?'

'I don't know why you're so worried about it, Daisy. Take a leaf out of Lily's book and relax,' Mum says, raising her eyebrows at me.

'Yeah, relax . . .' I say. I must be hiding my anxiety better than I realized. God, it's feeling too real. Kitchen supplies, forms to fill in, days disappearing before my eyes. It's so out of control. I wish I could go back in time and tell myself that this so-called 'independence', deliberately distancing myself from my mum and especially from Daisy, isn't really what I want. It's what I think I should want. But I don't want it — not yet, anyway.

'Are we ready to go?' Daisy asks, impatiently.

'Yes, let's hit the road,' I say, blowing a kiss to Crystal

as we head out the door. She meows back at me like she understands.

Between the clip-clops of Daisy's shoes beside me, I'm lost in thought. Every time I try to tell Daisy about Cal, she reminds me of another reason why I shouldn't. She'll take it as some kind of personal insult. Some kind of slight against her. That he's with me, instead of her.

For two people who have been compared all our lives, we are prickly about being in competition with each other. It's been the unspoken, unaddressed friction between us since we were old enough to know it was happening. And, truthfully, I'm not used to being the winner. I don't want to get into it with her, because I don't want her to feel cornered into saying stuff that'll make me feel bad.

All of a sudden she looks at me quizzically, like she can sense what's going on inside my brain. 'Daisy . . .' I begin, as we walk past the row of shops containing the good butcher and the bad fishmonger and the empty shop where the post office used to be.

'Mmm?'

'It's cool that we're not competing for the same stuff anymore, isn't it?' I've decided this is a useful tactic in talking about the Cal situation.

'Yeah, I guess . . .' Daisy furrows her brow. 'It's not nativity plays and rounders teams anymore.'

'Like our paths . . . our tastes . . . have diverged,' I say, awkwardly gesturing with my hands to indicate a road splitting in two directions.

'Sure, yeah, I get it. Like you're the arty one, I'm the sciencey one. I'm sporty, you like making stuff.'

'Right,' I say, sensing now is the time, this very moment, to tell her about Cal.

'We have different friends, different crushes. Not that we'd be going for the same guys, though.' She shrugs so casually, like it's nothing, like it wouldn't even cross her mind. I don't know what to say. It's like, it's not just *unlikely* but *impossible*.

I look at her. 'Wouldn't we?'

Daisy suddenly looks trapped. 'I mean . . . I didn't mean . . . I just meant that, like, we like different guys, which is true, right?'

It's not, really. But I decide to let her off the hook. 'Sure.'

I can hear my heart pounding angrily in my chest. It strikes me as so unfair that I have to feel everything so intensely, when she gets to be casual. All her anxieties are just a performance – a way to get people to reassure her of what she already knows (that she's amazing). I can't tell anyone how I feel for exactly the same reason (that I'm not).

I want to tell her about Cal just to prove her wrong, as

much for revenge as anything. But I won't have my evening ruined before it's begun.

As we're waiting for the traffic lights to change, a poster across the road catches my eye and takes my mind away from Daisy. It's in the same style as the racist poster, but this one has a different theme: a rainbow LBGTQIA+ pride flag with a big black cross through it and 'NO PRIDE IN WESTON BAY' emblazoned across it. I know it's my imagination, but for a split second one of the people illustrated on the poster looks like Cassie.

Seaforth, the bigger, busier town, has its own (admittedly small) Pride event and there was talk of setting up a Weston Bay version next year. I let out a little gasp of fury and feel my cheeks start to burn.

I think about running over and tearing it down, but something about Daisy being there stops me. She'll read something into it. I'll get it on the way home.

I meet Cal at the Crown because they do the cheapest pints and neither the cinema nor the ice-cream stand pay us enough to live luxuriously. Trying to put the whole poster thing out of my mind, I kiss him on the lips when we meet. He looks gorgeous, unshaven and slightly tanned from his morning in the sun. And more than that, he looks happy to see me, happy that I'm there and that I'm kissing him. Happiness is enough. Happiness is straightforward, and in a summer where I feel like nothing is straightforward, it is a relief to have an anchor.

I go up to the bar to get us drinks, and while I'm waiting to be served, someone sidles up to me. I glance to the side and realize it's none other than Molly.

'Hi Lily!' She throws her arms around me with surprising enthusiasm.

'Hi Molly, how are you?' I ask, before turning back to the barman to order.

'I'm great! Just out with my brother who's home from uni, we're so bored at home.' She pauses for a second. 'Hey, who are you here with?' There's something about the way she's asking the question that means she knows something, though I can't tell what.

'Um, just a guy I'm seeing,' I say as I tap my card on the machine. I wonder what Molly's up to.

'Oh! I thought I saw you come in with someone else.'

'Who?'

'No one, just this kinda hot, tall guy with dark hair that I see around sometimes,' she says, batting the whole subject away dismissively.

I want to laugh out loud but I manage not to. There's something simultaneously so absurd and hilarious about her, how pathetic and narrow-minded she is. In her mind it's impossible that the person she saw me with could also be the person I'm dating.

'Yeah . . .' I say, suppressing a smile. 'Well, you and your brother have a fun night.'

I walk back over to our table, put the glasses down and flick a glance towards the bar to see if Molly's looking. I see that she is, so instead of sitting in the chair opposite Cal, I slide into the booth next to him, slip my arm around his shoulder and kiss him. When I pull away after a moment, I look back to the bar and see Molly staring open-mouthed. I wink at her and return to my seat.

'Uh, thanks for the pint,' Cal says, slightly bewildered.

'No problem,' I say, smiling. 'How was your shift?'

'Hellish. The air conditioner broke in one of the screens. It was absolute chaos. I can't believe it happened on my shift, on one of the hottest days of the year. But I'm here now,' he replies brightly, taking a sip from his glass. 'I've truly earned these drinks, I'm telling you.'

'I'll drink to that,' I say. We sip our icy-cold pints for a moment.

I open my mouth to say something when someone in a teal sequinned top and denim cut-off shorts catches my eye at the bar. I squint in confusion. Cassie?

Cal stands up. 'Hey, man!' He's clapping Jack on the back. Now this I was not expecting.

Cassie looks over and seems as surprised as me. She

carries her and Jack's drinks over and sets them down on the table. 'Uh, this is a coincidence,' she says, hugging me with great enthusiasm.

'Not exactly . . .' Jack says, looking shifty.

'We never get the same evening off so thought we would take advantage of it,' says Cal.

'And of course I wasn't going to cancel seeing Cassie,' Jack adds quickly.

'A surprise double date . . .' I say weakly. I guess a double date can be my new thing today, since I haven't come up with anything else.

There's no reason why it should be awkward – we've all met before. But the element of surprise has clearly thrown Cassie and me off a little. We're pulling awkward faces at each other across the table, which probably doesn't help.

'Hey, have you noticed those posters around town?' Cassie asks before taking a sip of her beer.

'The weird old-timey ones?' Cal asks.

'Yeah, those ones,' Cassie says. It's clearly been weighing on her mind all day. 'They're fucked up.'

'Some fascist bullshit masquerading as nostalgia,' Cal says, shaking his head.

'I wonder who put them up,' Jack says, and as he says it, I look around the pub and think that they could be right here, right now. They're probably not, but still. They're somewhere.

'I guess I hadn't really realized how bad things can be here,' I say, looking down at my drink. It's like the people I love aren't safe in the place they live.

'Not to minimize specific stuff here, but it feels like that's the way the world is going. It's scary. It's shit,' says Cal.

'I feel like I want to *do* something about those disgusting posters,' Cassie says, her jaw set and determined. 'But I haven't figured out what yet.'

'Let me know when you do,' I say, looking her in the eye.

We sit in silence for a moment, no one sure what to say, but before long Cal reaches out and squeezes my hand and we're all back into a comfortable back and forth, talking about films and travel and our families and our lives and TV shows that make us laugh and I'm just really glad to be here with him and Cassie and, I guess, Jack too.

'Another?' Cal asks as the hands of the big clock above the door sweep past eleven.

'What do you think, Cassie?' I ask her.

Cassie shrugs. 'Why not? Keep the double-date dream alive.'

Jack goes up with him, leaving me and Cassie alone at the table. 'Did you know about this?!' I ask her.

'No! I don't get why they didn't mention it? Guys are weird.'

'Still, it was kind of fun.'

'Yeah! And a good excuse to see you without even making a plan to see you,' she says, with a faux-devilish cackle. She sets me off laughing, and when Cal and Jack return with our drinks, we're in fits of inexplicable giggles.

We hold it together while the four of us chat but every so often we'll catch each other's eye and have to suppress a laugh. Maybe a double date isn't so bad if it means I get to hang out with Cassie.

'So,' Cal says, looking in Cassie's direction. 'Are you going to uni in September, too?'

'Nope! I'm doing an art foundation course at the college. Not that my parents are happy about that . . .' As she takes a sip of her drink with her right hand, I realize Jack's hand is resting on her left. *Oh*, I think. Before Cal has a chance to reply, I drape my arm around his shoulder. If he shakes it off I'll be absolutely mortified, but I still feel compelled to do it.

'Sounds like a pretty decent prospect to me?' says Cal, reaching up and squeezing my hand. Phew.

'I think they would prefer I learned how to manage the family business . . .' Cassie says evenly, although she's clearly bothered by it. I'm never sure with Cassie whether she wants to talk about stuff or if I'm intruding. Maybe I'm not the only one keeping things to myself.

'Nah, you seem like you have the soul of an artist,' Cal says with a cute smile.

'I'll tell my mum that, maybe it'll make her feel better.' Cassie laughs. She pecks Jack on the cheek and I wonder how to up the ante with Cal. *What am I doing? Literally what is wrong with me? Why am I trying to compete, trying to perform?* It's not like I'm *not* enjoying spending time as a four, but there's definitely something about this dynamic that's making me prickle. Making me feel like I have something to prove.

'Lily?' Cassie says like it's not the first time she said it. I realize I completely zoned out.

'Shall we get going?' Cal asks.

As we get up to go, I catch sight of our reflection in a big mirror on the other side of the pub. People like Molly trying to make me feel that the mere idea of someone who looks anything like me going out with someone like Cal is absurd, does sometimes make me wonder if it *is* absurd. But when I see us together it just looks kind of normal. In my worst moments I find myself wondering if maybe everyone's right, but I know, I *know* deep down that they're not. That I'm fine just the way I am. That I deserve to be happy and to have what I want.

We all say goodbye outside the pub, and as Jack and Cassie walk off, I try not to wonder if they're going home together.

At night on the high street, away from the pubs, it feels like a ghost town.

'We could be the only people here,' says Cal, looking over his shoulder as we walk.

'That would be equal parts creepy . . . and hot,' I reply, stopping to draw him into a kiss. We lean against the shutters of the bookshop and I wonder how many of their books I would have to read before I found one where a girl like me is allowed to kiss a guy like Cal.

We stay there a long time, his body pressed against mine, before breaking away and wordlessly carrying on walking. It feels like this is something that happens to someone else, not to me, but it *is* happening to me. We walk hand in hand to the point where we separate to go home.

'Hey, what do you think about . . . coming over to mine next time?' Cal asks, and I guess I know what he's really asking.

My heart beats a bit faster. I knew this was on the horizon but it still feels like a *moment*, you know? My . . . first time. 'Yes,' I say decisively, even though I'm kinda nervous at the thought of having sex. With Cal I feel so sure of myself. So in control. Besides, I know that if I show any kind of uncertainty he'll say we have to wait until I'm sure, and I *am*. I'm so attracted to him that I'm risking my relationship with Daisy. I'm invested. What else is there to it?

'Are you sure?' He raises an eyebrow and reaches out for my hand.

'I'm sure,' I tell him emphatically. But I feel the anxiety start to settle in my chest, not as much as usual, but just the creeping beginnings of panic. I take long, deep breaths in and out, until I feel on top of it and I'm able to carry on. I feel powerful for being able to control it, even just this once. To avert the full-blown panic.

'Alright, we can figure out the date another time, no need to lock it down now,' he says. 'I don't want you to feel pressured or anything.'

'No, of course.'

I draw him to me and rest my forehead on his. He looks back at me, our faces close together. 'You're such a funny one,' he says. 'I never have any idea what's going on in there.' *You and me both*, I think. He puts his hand on the top of my head, before stroking my hair and giving me one last peck on the lips before we go our separate ways.

As I make my way through the quiet streets, something bright catches my eye under a street lamp. Another poster, this one slightly billowing in the breeze, only pasted down at the top and the bottom. With a resolve that mounts with every passing day, I get out my keys and slash it through the middle before ripping each half off its pasted strip. There is no satisfaction in it. Everything is overshadowed by the knowledge that someone agrees with this poster.

The closer I get to home, the more I sense I'm not alone. I wonder if I'm being followed, and as soon as I have that thought, that back-of-the-neck prickle feeling, I become so certain of it that I'm too scared to look over my shoulder and check. Did someone see me tearing down the poster? I'm a slow walker but I slow even more to see if I can hear footsteps or if it's in my imagination, before hearing a swift, clipped step behind me. I speed up again, almost running to my front door, and as I put my key in the lock, I hear someone shout, 'Wait for me!'

I realize it's my sister. Relief floods through me even though I don't know exactly who or what I was afraid of.

'Jesus Daisy, you scared me!'

Daisy pauses for a minute as she leans against the floral wallpaper in the hall and unbuckles her sandals. There's a look in her eye that I only catch for a minute before she heads upstairs without saying goodnight.

It's only then that I start to wonder how long she'd been on my tail, and what she'd seen.

# CHAPTER EIGHT

'How was the cinema?' I ask Daisy over breakfast the next morning. It's our mum's turn to work on a Saturday, so we're home alone. Daisy hasn't said much to me all morning. Everything is tense – I'm scared if I put my knife down too loudly it will be enough to break whatever deathly quiet we've settled into.

'It was fine,' she says.

'And cocktails at the Lighthouse?'

'They were fine, too,' she says. She stirs her cereal pointlessly and doesn't look at me.

'Oh, good . . .' I say, waiting for her to ask me something about my evening, or even look up from her bowl. I hate this so much.

'I would tell you that the guy I fancy wasn't at the cinema,' she says, pausing. 'But you already knew that, right?'

'What do you mean?' I ask as casually as I can, in a desperate attempt to avoid, postpone, delay what's next.

'Come on, Lily.' She rolls her eyes in exasperation.

'This is why you've been so secretive lately. You know you're doing something wrong. It's not in your nature, so you're creeping around and being weird rather than just being honest about it!' She drops her spoon down onto the table with a clatter.

I swallow, not sure what to say next. 'I didn't mean to upset you. I really didn't, I promise. It just kind of happened!' Uh-oh. Telling Daisy the truth about Cal just turned into my new thing for the day.

'Oh, that's OK then,' she says, mockingly.

'I tried to tell you! Loads of times!'

'Well you didn't try very hard then, did you?'

'That's because every time I did you would say something presumptuous or patronizing and I wouldn't know how to deal with it!'

'Don't try to change the subject! You lied to my face!'

I don't want this to spiral. There have been so many near-fights between us in the last couple years that I've carefully avoided, but there's no easy way out of this. I feel a slight panic set in. 'I mean . . . it's not like he was your boyfrie—'

'That's not the point! You knew I liked him and you just went behind my back and asked him out and kept it a secret! You were deliberately sneaky. This isn't like you . . .' Daisy trails off. 'You're not even bothered about meeting guys. You've *never* been bothered about meeting guys! Not for years! So why are you suddenly so intent on stealing the one guy you knew I really liked?'

'I didn't do any sneaking or any stealing! We met in the pub and he just asked me out! He's hot, he's kind, he's interested in me, it has nothing to do with you!'

'*He* asked *you* out?' Daisy says instantly, as if she couldn't keep it in for a second longer.

'Yeah, Daisy, I know that's hard for you to believe.' I roll my eyes.

'That's not what I meant,' she says, sternly, but behind the set of her jaw there's a furtiveness, like an animal evading capture.

'What did you mean then?'

'I . . .' She gapes like a goldfish.

'Right.'

'No, it's just . . .'

'What?' I urge her to speak, but she doesn't, she's just sitting there trying to formulate what she knows she can't say in a way that's more palatable and allows her to maintain the moral high ground. She's looking at me, waiting for me to fill the gap for her, waiting for me to let her off the hook. But I won't do it. Not this time.

'It's just . . . not like you.' She shrugs.

'OK, it's not like me, but why is that disturbing you so much? Don't I have the right to change and maybe even

141

once in a while do something that you don't expect?'

Daisy lets out a noise of frustration and picks up the cushion on the empty chair next to her, pummelling it into shape.

'We never compete for guys!' Daisy says, finally. 'I hate it! I just really hate it!'

I stare at her, genuinely baffled. How can she not see this? 'We never compete because you always get what you want, no questions asked. Remember Joel Edwards? Patrick Saunders when we were on holiday in France? Jack Calder from our drama group? And let's not forget Tom Greenwell! One after another I just had to watch as guys I got on with, who I felt a spark with, suddenly became your latest must-have boy as soon as I said a word about them. I was so nervous, so scared, and I pushed through it to talk to them because I liked them, and then you just swept in. Cal is the first guy who's preferred me to you and you can't handle it.'

'No, that's not it, it's just—' she babbles, reddening.

'It's just that you never expected someone *you* liked to be interested in me, because why would they be when they could have you, right? You've never been able to get your head around the thought that beauty isn't some kind of one-size-fits-all thing. You're pretty, there's no doubt about it! I've never, ever said you're not. But it's like it's never crossed your mind that I could be too? I get that's how a lot of people look at me, but I need better from my own sister.'

I know that look. She doesn't know what to say to me. She thought she knew how everything worked, knew our places in the world, and now she's finding out she doesn't.

'That's not true! I don't think that!' Daisy is indignant.

'Really? You *really* don't think that?' I ask her. 'Don't pretend you don't know that it's how people see us and it's the way we've been made to see ourselves.'

'It's not like I have it easy all the time, you know,' she says.

'I'm not saying you do. I'm just saying that, at this point in our lives, guys have a track record of going for you. And you love that there's *something* that sets you apart from me.'

I wonder if she's ever really thought about it at all before now. If she ever considered how her constant assumptions and judgements made me feel. 'Look,' I say. 'I get that you're annoyed because it feels like I've taken something from you, but I haven't. You didn't even know his name. And besides, he's a whole person in his own right! You don't just get to decide what he does or what choices he makes just because you saw him first.'

She's looking at me resolutely. 'It's not about that, it's about the fact you didn't tell me.' So this is her tactic.

'Well I might have done if I thought you were capable of really listening. All you do is project your image of who I am onto me.'

'You let me keep bringing him up and you knew the whole time! I saw you two making out on the street! This is a proper *thing* and I had no idea about any of it!' She looks like a petulant, disgruntled child. 'I don't get why you stopped talking to me.'

'I didn't *mean* to stop talking to you—' I protest, wanting to say more but not sure how to.

'So are you going to keep seeing him?' Daisy snaps.

Cal is really special – I feel so sure of myself with him. I've never had that before – usually when I fancy someone, I'm a nervous wreck. When I'm with Cal I'm not worried about anything beyond the here and now. He makes me forget about uni and how I'm leaving everything behind so soon. 'Yes. I like him.'

'Ugh, sure,' she says, exasperated.

'So you want me to just stop seeing him and then what? Tell him he has to go out with you to somehow rebalance the universe so the thin twin gets the ending she deserves?'

'It's not about that!'

'I don't get what it is about then! You're just not used to not getting your way, and more than anything you're not used to me getting something you want. You've never seen me as a threat. I'm not just an inferior version of you, I'm me. I'm a whole person.'

She rolls her eyes but I can tell it's hit home a bit. 'I *know* that.' I wonder if she really does know it, if she really has thought about it at all before now. Maybe she never had to.

'OK, so what's the problem?'

'You never tell me anything anymore,' Daisy says, her voice burning with a kind of anger that I find shocking. 'There's been something going on with you for months now and once upon a time you would have confided in me but now you just don't share anything, like I wouldn't understand. Like I'm too dumb to understand your big, deep, sensitive life. You think I make assumptions about you? Well what about you making assumptions about me? You didn't even tell me that we weren't going to be together anymore. You just made a decision and went ahead with it.'

'What the fuck? What are you even talking about?'

She swallows, her eyes wide. 'We had a plan to stay together. We were meant to be going to uni together. That was what we were meant to be doing. And you just, out of nowhere, decided to change your mind without telling me.'

I feel like she's hit me. I just look at her. 'I . . . figured it was time to live my life and for you to live yours!' I say finally, blinking in disbelief. 'I didn't know that us going to the same uni was, like, a done deal for you! I didn't know

I was locked into it! You're always on at me about being more independent and now that's what I'm *trying* to do you don't like it?'

'You never talked to me about it at all! It was me and you against the world until you went to college and replaced me with Cassie, and I thought we were going to be back to how it used to be when we went to uni and then you just went and decided for us that it wasn't meant to be.'

This has been simmering under the surface for her and I had no idea. I really didn't.

'I thought it was for the best for us! I thought it was what you wanted! You don't need me around! You just don't – you find it so easy to make friends and meet people, if anyone would need to have the other around it would be me! I thought I was doing you a favour!'

'You think you're the only one with fears and worries and it means you completely overlook everyone else's! How many times have you rejected my invites out?! How many times have I burst into your room and started a conversation with you? Sometimes I think the only reason you even applied to uni was to get away from me.'

Before I can respond she turns away from me and runs up to her room, puts on her garden centre uniform and leaves the house with the necessary slamming of the door. Even with her gone I feel like my adrenaline is making the atmosphere fizz furiously. *Me? Replacing her with Cassie?* She never needed me! It was always me clinging on to her, wasn't it? Her, more secure, more confident, more popular, always finding it easy to make friends. *I* needed *her*, until I decided it was healthier for me to, you know, detach. Because she kept talking about how I wouldn't! I don't feel like I understand anything, and I can barely hear myself think over the sound of blood rushing in my ears.

I've got to get out of here. In a daze, I hastily dress in my leggings, sports bra and T-shirt, and pull my trainers on without undoing the laces. I swipe my keys from the shelf, slamming the door behind me, and hit the road, trying to get out of my head and into my body with a slow, steady jog.

I stew as I run. I keep turning it all over in my mind, looking at it all from different angles. The way Daisy assumed I'm just not in the same game as her at all . . . All these people – even my own sister – seem to think they know so much about me just from the size of my body. I feel like I have to work so hard to keep on top of my body image, but I *do* work on it. And that's enough for Cal. And Cassie.

As I run under a railway bridge on the far side of town, I see a row of posters on the dark brick wall of the tunnel and my thoughts instantly switch to the promise I made Cassie to tear them down. I may be a terrible sister by all accounts, but I won't be a terrible friend. I slow my pace and cross the road, taking my keys out of my pocket. I run the sharpest edge of my house key along the top of one of the posters, unsticking the glue and letting it flop down before pulling the whole thing off and scrunching it in a ball that I kick along to the next one. When I've done all four, I gather up the scrunched-up posters and carry them in my arms to the nearest bin. I shove them in and set off again, running running running.

*Where am I going?* I stop in the middle of a deserted road, panting, doubled over with fatigue. Actually, *where am I?* I go to check Google Maps before realizing that I left my phone at home. I wander about, a mixture of aimless and frustrated. I guess if I get lost or kidnapped by angry fascist poster designers it'll mean I don't have to deal with Daisy again. I wouldn't have to go to university and leave Cassie behind. Or maybe, rather than a blessing, it would be more of an instant karma type thing. You know, for lying to my twin. I feel like I should be having this meltdown in the middle of a really intense rain storm, but the lovely seaside weather remains temperate as I burn inside.

Then I see it. The corner shop where we always buy fireworks for Bonfire Night. From there, it's only a couple of minutes' walk to Cassie's semi-detached house on a quiet street in Seaforth. I was running to *Cassie*. Maybe Jogging Lily does know what she's about.

I press the doorbell, praying she's home, praying for comfort and praying for some familiarity. The door swings open.

'What happened to *you*?' Cassie asks, eyeing my still-red cheeks, my sweaty ponytail and my very-much-not-chic-athleisure outfit with confusion.

'I had to clear my head . . .' I say, stepping into the hall.

'Who is it?' Cassie's dad calls from the kitchen.

'Lily!'

'I should have known!' Carl calls back. Cassie's done a marginally better job than me of keeping up with her old friends but . . . it really is just me and her a lot of the time.

'Hi!' I call, as brightly as I can manage. We enter the kitchen to Carl Palmer cracking eggs into a huge bowl, the top of his bald head looking . . . well, I suppose the polite term would be sun-blushed.

'You've got good timing! I was just making me and Cassie some pancakes before I get back to the gardening!'

'Promise me you'll wear some sunscreen this time?' Cassie asks, wearily.

'Why, am I looking pink?' Carl grabs a big spoon and looks in the back of it like a mirror, craning to see the top of his skull. 'Bloody hell!'

'I would love a pancake!' I call behind me, as Cassie drags me out of the kitchen and into the living room.

She plonks me down unceremoniously on the squishy sofa and lies at one end with her feet across my lap. We're watching the channel that only shows wedding dress programmes. Normally we would be yelling 'vile!', 'grim!', 'how is that different to the last one?' and very, very infrequently, a reverential 'oooh!' on the rare occasion they try on something that isn't completely disgusting. But today we watch in silence.

Once the adverts start, she sits upright and gestures for us to switch positions. 'So what's up?'

'Nothing's up . . .' I lie. Badly.

She rolls her eyes. 'Something's up. You *ran* here.'

'Can't I run places?'

'You and I both know . . . you don't do that.' She fixes me with a serious stare. I wonder where to begin, but deep down I know I don't really want to talk to Cassie about Cal. Not even about me and Daisy fighting because of Cal. Good job there's all the other stuff to tell her about!

'Ugh!' Finally, I flop back onto the arm of the sofa. What am I here for if not comfort and advice? This is what best friends are for. Reassurance. Unconditional love. Just at that moment, Carl nudges open the living room door with his hip, carrying a tray.

'Pancakes for the ladies!'

'Thank you so much, this looks amazing,' I say, eyeing the little jug of maple syrup and the fresh, fluffy stack.

'Now, I'm off to find a big hat before I go outside again . . .'

We eat in silence for a moment, letting the ads for steam mops and juicers and inflatable beds pop up and fade away before our eyes.

'I had a fight with Daisy. It started as just like a . . . stupid thing, you know?' I brush off the origin of the fight as if it never happened. I wish. I really don't want Cassie to know that Cal was Daisy's crush. I know she'll think it wasn't cool for me to keep that from Daisy. 'But then it kind of escalated and she accused me of, like, abandoning her?'

'Huh?'

'Well, first she said I replaced her with you – absurd – and then she said I abandoned her by changing my uni plans and accepting the offer from Leeds.'

'That's pretty harsh of her,' Cassie says, chewing thoughtfully.

'Yeah! That's what I thought . . .'

'I mean, on the one hand, taking something small and making it into a massive thing is very not cool. I'm sorry that it upset you so much you felt the need to *run* here. On the other, you and Daisy have been gearing up for a fight for ages. I'm honestly impressed you managed to keep the peace this long.'

'I mean I guess so – but replacing her? Really?!'

Cassie looks at me out of the corner of her eye. 'So you don't think you did?'

'No, obviously not!'

'But do you get why she would see it like that?'

I sigh. 'I mean . . . no?' I think for a moment. 'Or maybe . . . yes, but I hadn't thought of it before? But it's not like she's perfect herself,' I say, thinking about all the times she's made me feel uncomfortable because of my body.

'Oh?' Cassie asks, inquisitively.

However much I mean it, suddenly I feel disloyal. No matter what, talking shit about Daisy feels wrong. 'Ha, just kidding. She's perfect. Hey, the brides are back,' I say, gesturing at the TV. Cassie looks at me sideways but doesn't press any further.

We hear the front door open and close.

'Hi!'

'Hi, Mum,' Cassie calls.

'Hi, Tracy,' I call so she knows I'm there.

'Oh! Hi, Lily,' says Tracy as she appears from the hall.

'Everything under control?' I ask her.

'As far as I can tell.' Tracy shrugs brightly. 'I haven't

seen you away from the stand for a long time, Lily!'

'Yeah, it's true! Thank you so much for giving me a job, I really appreciate it.'

'Nonsense! I was happy to. How's all your uni prep going?'

'Oh, fine,' I say, hoping we don't have to talk about this for too long.

'I bet your mum's proud of you and your sister,' she says warmly. I can feel Cassie's body language change next to me. A defensive turn of the head away from our conversation. 'Both going to university, going to get degrees.'

'I mean, I guess.'

'Such good girls.' She smiles ruefully. 'Now, I'm going to relax in the garden. Don't you two want to get outside? Instead of being cooped up in here?'

'We spend more than enough time outside, Mum.' Cassie sighs.

Once Tracy has joined her husband in the garden and is sufficiently out of earshot, I turn to Cassie. 'What was that about?'

'Just the latest in my parents' attempts to guilt trip me about my choices.'

'Oh, shit, they're still not OK with it?'

'Nope. I think if I was going to uni that would be one thing, but for me to a) not apply to uni and b) say I don't want to work at Palmer's forever? That's too far. They just don't get it.'

'But you're doing an art foundation course. That's not nothing?'

'I know that. You know that. But *they* don't know that.' Cassie cocks her head in the direction of the garden. 'They *disapprove*.'

'Ugh, I'm sorry.'

'It's not your fault. You do everything right,' she says, playfully poking at my foot with hers. 'It's just a bit annoying, that's all. I wish they got it. I wish they supported me in this, you know? I had to properly fight for them to even let me do it in the first place – you know they wanted me to do business studies or something dull like that. They see it as me letting the side down in not supporting the family business after they completely rebuilt it. Like, yeah, that's amazing and everything, but it doesn't mean *I* want to carry it on? At least, not to the extent that I'm gonna study business or accountancy or something?'

'Yeah . . . I'm sorry,' I say guiltily. I realize that my mum didn't put up *any* opposition to my plans, didn't try to change my mind about anything at all. Now I would *definitely* feel bad about sharing my uni anxieties with Cassie.

'It's not *your* fault. They're just obsessed with the idea

that I'm going to be unemployed and living here forever. As if that's what I want!'

'Your mum might be the only person in the world who thinks me doing an art history degree is, like, an incredibly smart, strategic thing to do – I should keep her around for pep talks,' I joke.

Cassie smiles weakly, but I can tell she's not happy. 'I know they love me unconditionally, blah blah et cetera, I just wish they were like . . . fully on board with my shit?'

'They're just protective, right? It's scary and unstable to be an artist! You're heading into a scary and unstable career. Of course they want you to be happy, but I guess for them, happiness looks like stability.'

She nods decisively. 'Come on, let me do your nails.'

Not wanting to talk about Big Life Stuff anymore, Cassie paints my nails, gently layering on the vibrant red nail varnish and making sure she leaves that tiny, imperceptible gap around the cuticle that makes it look neat and fresh.

'What can I say? I'm a woman of many talents,' she says, admiring her handiwork. As I look at her looking at my nails, all glossy and red, I can't help but feel bad that I didn't know how she felt about this stuff with her parents. It makes me wonder what else she's not telling me.

Spending time with Cassie always makes me feel better, somehow. But even so, I walk home under a bleak grey cloud of irritation. Everything good in my life feels like it's being tarnished by other people's bullshit. Daisy assuming a guy like Cal wouldn't have any interest in a girl like me. Accusing me of abandonment when I'm actually terrified of the choice I made. And if I do leave home, this town that I love, when I come back it will have been taken over by horrifyingly racist, homophobic human beings who probably hate ice cream like they hate everything else good in this world. And what is it with Daisy always implying that I'm spending too much time with Cassie? It's not my fault everyone seems dull in comparison to her.

# CHAPTER NINE

'So she's still not talking to you, huh?' Cassie asks as I hold the base of the candy-striped parasol.

'Nope,' I say, squinting up at her in the early morning sunshine. 'Not if she can help it.'

Cassie sighs sympathetically. 'Well, I guess you just have to wait it out. It can't last forever.'

'I don't know . . .' I murmur. 'But thankfully Mum knows to stay out of it. She seems to have this belief that it'll blow over . . .'

'It will! You're *twins*. Hey, at least we know what today's new thing is going to be!' Cassie waggles her eyebrows at me. I swallow hard.

'Yea . . .' It's not that I'm not looking forward to my *hot* date with Cal later, I'm just, well, nervous. Not nervous about . . . the thing. The actual sex part. Just nervous about everything around it.

'You feeling OK about it?' Cassie asks.

'Yeah, sure!' I say, brightly.

'You don't sound convinced.'

I sigh. 'Is it . . . going to hurt?'

'Maybe. I'm not going to tell you that it's not.'

'Guhhhh,' I say, tipping my head back in defeat.

'Don't wind yourself up about it too much because then you'll panic and it'll probably hurt more because you're stressed,' she says, resting reassuring hands on my shoulders. 'You're meant to enjoy it, but don't worry if it's not like amazing and perfect first time, that's like . . . very normal.'

'OK, I hear you,' I say, as confidently as possible. 'I just find the thought of being, like, *fully naked* in front of someone quite . . . a lot? You know?'

'Yeah.' She shrugs thoughtfully. 'It is. But . . . you know there's nothing wrong with your body, right?'

'Right,' I say, a little distracted. 'It's just a whole new frontier. I guess I won't really know how I'll feel until I'm in the moment . . .'

In general, I tiptoe around the subject with Cassie. Part of me wants to know if she's had sex with Jack yet, and the other part wants to bury its head in the sand and never have to know. But I am glad I can awkwardly hit her up for advice.

Lucky for me, we're not going to get a moment's peace today. The queues are long from the moment we open. Everyone knows it's the last really hot day of the year. The heatwave has been all over the news and word is that the temperature is going to drop overnight. But being here, during a hectic work day, is better than being home with Daisy. It feels safe just being around Cassie. I can breathe properly, and I don't have to be constantly on my guard.

'Fancy a drink?' Cassie asks as we're closing up for the day. A knot forms in my stomach at the thought of saying no to her.

'I can't . . .' I say, slowly. 'Remember?'

She hits herself on the forehead. 'Duh! Your romantic evening! How about this weekend though?'

'Yeah, definitely!'

'And we should do something a little different at some point too! Let's go to the park and have a picnic or something? Or the beach! Seaforth for a change of scenery? For tomorrow we can just grab a drink?' Cassie asks. 'Unless you think you'll still be at Cal's then . . .'

'No way, I'm not going to sleep over,' I say, realizing the idea hadn't even crossed my mind. 'Tomorrow afternoon is perfect.'

'You don't think it's weird, right?'

'What?' I ask.

'I guess I mean . . . like, us spending all week working together then hanging out together on the weekend, too?'

'Nah. Even if it is I don't think I care that much,' I say,

shrugging. I think of my horrible breakfast with Molly.

'Me either,' she says, squinting and turning her face up to the sun. She takes her baseball cap off and lets her hair gently bounce back into its usual shape after having been flattened by the hat. She's so beautiful.

As we're winding down for the day, Señor Mango Sorbet and Lady Red Plum appear, grimacing and looking apologetic, asking if they're too late. We let them off. We're nice like that.. 'Ever drawn them?' I ask Cassie.

'Weirdly, no,' she replies. 'Maybe today's the day.'

'It's been a while,' I say to them.

'He's been working too hard! Hasn't been able to leave at a decent hour,' Lady Red Plum says, shaking her head. 'Even today I've only got him for now and then he's out at some colleague or other's leaving drinks.'

'Well, we're happy you're both back. Customer retention is *very* important to us here at Palmer's,' Cassie says with a wink before serving them their usual and watching them wander off. There's something comforting about the familiarity. Like even if I won't be here to see it, everything will just carry on as usual in my absence. Even in the winter, Palmer's Ices does good business.

'Is your mum still internet dating?'

'Yes, there seems to be this one guy, though, rather than general dating. I think she's seeing him later on,' I say.

'Big night for romance in Weston Bay.' Cassie wiggles her eyebrows at me, suggestively, and maybe I'm imagining it but there's something in her eyes that doesn't quite match up.

'Yeah! And who can believe it's *me* doing the romance?'

'But you do really like him, right?' Cassie asks.

I'm taken aback a little. 'Yeah, sure, why not? Should I not?' I garble

'No, it's not that . . .' Cassie reaches out and puts her hand on my arm. 'I just wanted to make sure.'

Before long, I find myself walking to the flat Cal shares with a couple of other guys. I'm kind of excited to see him without the Daisy drama holding me back. Now it's out in the open, I'm free to just enjoy myself, no longer weighed down by all the sneakery. I mean yeah, I'm still dealing with the fallout of previous sneakery, but I'll deal with that later. Right now I'm just basking in the joy of dating someone who's cool and strong enough to know their own mind, who's kind and interesting, who likes me for who I am.

I check my reflection in the window of a parked car a couple of houses down. I'm wearing a brilliant-white T-shirt tucked into a pleated leopard-print skirt – it was a strategic choice: cute . . . but easy to get on and off. I tuck my hair behind my ear, then untuck it again, then tie my hair in a ponytail, then let it down again, exactly like it was before I started messing around with it. I almost jump out of my skin when the window starts rolling down.

'Oh my god! I'm so sorry!' I say to the woman peering back at me from the inside of the car. 'I didn't know anyone was there!'

'Don't worry about it.' She beams, squinting at me in the early evening light. 'I just wanted to reassure you that you look beautiful. Keep your hair down, like that.'

'Oh! Thank you,' I say, blushing.

'Alright if I drive off now? You done using my window as a mirror?' she asks, kindly.

'Yes, of course! Sorry, it's so cringe, I feel so vain!'

'Don't worry about it!' she says. 'Have a nice evening!' With that, she drives off. I'm half mortified, half touched.

I knock on the door and am somehow surprised when Cal answers it, still discombobulated from being caught out in my vanity.

'Hey!' Cal says, drawing me into a hug on the doorstep. He's wearing a navy-blue striped apron and holding a big wooden spoon in his hand.

'I like your new look,' I say as he leads me into the flat.

'Ha, thanks,' he calls over his shoulder, heading back into the kitchen to put down the spoon and detangle himself from the apron. 'I hope you like spaghetti carbonara,' he says when he returns to kiss me in the living room.

'Who doesn't!'

'Uh, vegetarians, I guess?' Cal says good-naturedly, running a hand through his hair which is damp with kitchen sweat. 'It's nearly ready!'

His flat is small, but neat and well looked after, with piles of books everywhere and an acoustic guitar in one corner. The sofas are battered but the cushions on them are bright and stylish. My expectations for a home inhabited by three young men were . . . low, to be honest, but I'm pleasantly surprised.

I follow him into the kitchen which is, again, small, but has a little semicircle-shaped table set for two (you couldn't fit any more on it anyway) and a low candle burning. I blush, almost embarrassed by the thought of Cal making an effort for me.

'Well, this is nice . . .' I say, sitting at one of the rickety chairs. For a moment I'm convinced I'm going to break it. I don't break it. I never do break it, but the thought crosses my mind every time.

'I hope you say that about the pasta too! Sorry it's not much, I haven't been home from work that long.' He casts around distractedly, looking for something, before landing on a pair of tongs that he uses to extract the glistening strands from the pan and set them down onto two waiting plates. It smells amazing.

For someone only a year older than me, he's very good at, like . . . living in the world. There's no way I could be this comfortable living so far away from home, and all on my own. But then again, when I'm with Cal I feel so sure of myself. Maybe Leeds won't be so bad – if he can do it, why can't I?

'You didn't need to do this, you know,' I say, when we've finished.

'Yeah, I did. I mean, firstly I needed to eat dinner, and secondly I didn't want to make you feel like I only wanted you to come over for . . .' He trails off. 'You know.'

'Oh . . . that's OK. I don't think that.' He just . . . likes me. No angle, no ulterior motive. He just likes me.

He stands to put the dishes in the sink. 'I'll deal with those later. My housemates are away for the weekend on some camping trip. I told them there was no way I was sleeping in a tent in *these* temperatures.'

'Just the thought of it makes me feel sick,' I say, wiping my brow with the back of my hand. It is the last day of the heatwave, but part of me can't understand how it's just going to magically drop ten degrees overnight.

'Not much of an outdoorsy type?'

'Absolutely not,' I say, laughing. 'My sister Daisy is, though. And my mum, too, actually. She's kind of adventurous. Not sure what went so wrong with me in the gene pool.'

'Absolutely nothing went wrong with you,' he says, before kissing me.

For a moment I feel self-conscious of him touching my body, feeling the sweat through the back of my T-shirt, but I know he's safe and I know he knows what my body is like. He likes me. And my body is part of that. So I just let it happen and kiss him back. I take hold of the back of his head and feel the silkiness of his hair under my fingers.

Whatever nerves I'd worked up seem to have disappeared. It's *Cal*. He's safe. We work. 'Do you want to . . . ?' I trail off.

We head upstairs. His room doesn't have much stuff in it, which is unsurprising because he's on his travels. But like the rest of the house, it's well looked after.

'You . . . have done this before, right?' I ask him.

'Yeah.' He nods. 'Have you?'

'No . . . is that a problem?'

'No, it's not. It's just good to know, you know? Do you feel OK about it?'

'Yeah, I feel fine,' I say reflexively, which doesn't accurately convey my enthusiasm. 'More than fine. I don't know why I said fine.'

This kind, warm awkwardness continues onto the bed where we mess around, fumble and undress among nervous laughter and gentle encouragements.

And then . . . it happens. It just happens. I'm expecting it to hurt but it doesn't, not really. It's actually . . . pretty nice? I guess I've just heard one too many horror stories from girls in my class about incompetent idiot boys and thought that was the way it had to be. Should I ask Cassie what it was like with Jack? Was she more . . . into it than I am? And then I wonder if I should be thinking about Cassie at a time like this and force myself to return to the present moment, the one where I'm having sex for the first time.

When it's over, I lie there, and I feel so exposed. He's the first person to have seen me naked. To have seen my whole body. All of it. I feel so comfortable with him. But it's still there, that prickle of doubt.

'You look serious,' Cal says, propping himself up on his elbow and surveying me from his side of the bed.

'It's just weird, I guess.'

'What's weird?'

'I . . . can't really get my head around . . . this,' I say, gesturing between us. 'Like . . . why do you even like me? It's not like there aren't loads of other girls who are interested in you.' Maybe it's a bad thing that I feel so comfortable with Cal, because then I feel empowered to ask stupid questions like this.

'Jesus, Lily, I just like you, you know? It's not something you can really account for or explain. Sometimes you just see someone and think . . . *Yeah.*' He's looking at me with an expression of such confusion, like it hadn't crossed his mind that I would think this about myself. 'I'm not, like, *better* than you, you know that, right? You don't need to be so suspicious of me.'

'I guess . . . it's just weird sometimes, listening to other people.'

'Other people suck. Especially around here. You're great. Don't forget that.'

I sigh. 'Thank you. Sorry I'm being weird.'

He touches my stomach as I lie there. I don't flinch or try to move away. I just let his hand rest there, on the soft flesh.

Am I meant to feel different now I've had sex? I'm glad I got it out of the way before I go to university, I guess, but also I was never really that worried about it. It was more the whole . . . naked thing that was freaking me out. And there are *way* worse people to do it with than Cal. I might not be remotely experienced in that department, but I am sure he wasn't a bad place to start. It was good, and I feel lucky, even though everyone deserves a first time like that. I want to talk to Cassie about it because I talk to Cassie about everything. Or at least, I used to. There are more and more things that I'm not talking to her about these days.

When I get home, I'm surprised that the lights are on

downstairs. I thought everyone would be in bed by now.

*Please don't let it be Daisy. Please don't let it be Daisy. Please don't let it be Daisy*, I think as I turn my key in the lock. But of course it is. So much for twin telepathy.

'What have you been up to?' she asks from the kitchen doorway, holding a glass of water.

'Nothing. Just at Cal's,' I tell her.

She rolls her eyes, turns off the lights and turns to head upstairs.

'Is this how it's going to be forever now?' I ask, impatiently.

'You say that like it's my decision. You're the one who calls the shots around here,' she says, before walking up the stairs, leaving me standing in the dark hall.

# CHAPTER TEN

The next couple of weeks pass in a sun-soaked blur of kissing Cal, hanging out with Cassie and avoiding my sister. Cassie gives me a new thing for the day when she remembers. Some of my favourites include:

1. Sending food back when it's not right.
2. Going to a jazz, tap and modern fusion dance class with her.
3. Singing karaoke to a too-big crowd while far too sober.
4. Watching a Korean horror film with her.
5. Attempting to bake a caramel soufflé (and then putting out my first fire).
6. Learning how to distress and embroider my own jeans (badly).
7. Painting on a new kind of canvas.
8. Going to a poetry reading in a cafe I assumed I was definitely not cool enough to get into.
9. Taking a book out from the town library – and actually *reading* it.

10. Volunteering for the day at the local elderly
    community centre.

But I can't even focus on today's new thing because I
have made a catastrophic mistake. I looked at a calendar.
Only twelve days until results day. I kept counting and
re-counting the weeks as if they would magically change if
I counted them enough times, but they didn't, and when
I turned away from the wall I realized my chest felt tight
and I'd dug little crescent moons into the palms of my
hands.

Cassie will distract me. I can't wait to spend some time
with her away from the ice-cream stand. My mum offers to
give me a lift, but I say no way and tell her to have a chill
morning to herself. I pack the huge family picnic blanket
and take the bus to Seaforth where I meet Cassie at the bus
stop, who instantly wraps her arms around me and I breathe
her in and everything feels right. I squeeze her back, then it
strikes me that maybe I've held on a moment too long, so
I pull away. I move so fast that neither of us knows where
to look. Thankfully, we head for the corner shop to pick up
some goodies for our picnic, and things get back to normal.

Despite the (mercifully) slightly grey clouds, it's still
a Saturday and the beach is busy. We walk down the sand,
away from Seaforth's famously loud and colourful pier, to

a stretch of sand that's less densely populated. I spread out the picnic blanket with a flourish. We lower ourselves onto it in as dignified a manner as possible before taking all our delicious purchases out of the paper bag.

We congratulate ourselves on our excellent food choices for this picnic, a perfect array of olives, marinated anchovies, fancy bread, a couple of nice cheeses.

'Not to forget . . .' Cassie says, producing a plastic container from her bag, 'patties.'

'OMG, exciting!'

'They're not that exciting. Well, I guess my mum made them from scratch so credit where credit's due.'

'Exciting for me because I've never tried one before.'

'What?! You've never had a Jamaican patty?'

'I don't think so . . .'

'A perfect new thing of the day!' Cassie says, handing me one of the pleasingly sunny-yellow patties, dense and satisfying to hold in my hand, with its perfectly-crimped edges.

I take a bite. 'Perfection.'

'See what you've been missing out on your whole life?'

For dessert, we've chosen two swirly buns covered in white icing with a glacé cherry on top, like a glinting jewel.

'These are so perfect,' I say between mouthfuls.

'The concept cannot be improved upon. Can you

imagine if they tried to make these fancy? You would totally mess them up.'

'They are exactly as they should be,' I nod, sagely.

'I saw on Instagram earlier that Will and Clem from art are interrailing around Europe this summer. They're in Italy now and I think they just came from Greece, but you know what? I'm not even jealous!'

'You really mean that you'd rather work on the ice-cream stand and eat cheese on a cloudy beach with me than travel around Italy?' I say, fixing her with my most sceptical look.

'No *obviously* I would rather be messing around in the sunshine,' she replies, like I'm the stupidest person in the world. 'But what I mean is, like, given I am not at liberty to travel and spend extravagantly, hanging out with you all summer is not so bad. I'm not, like, mad about it, you know? I'm content as is – much like this excellent bun.'

I smile. It feels good to play a part in her summer.

'I know you've had the stuff with Daisy, but this summer's been kind of fun, too, right?'

'Yeah!' I say, gamely.

'I mean, you've really thrown yourself into this whole relationship thing with Cal!' Cassie says. She almost sounds impressed. 'Not usually something in the Lily Rose Comfort Zone!'

'Oh . . . I mean . . . I guess?' I furrow my brow instinctively. 'Haven't you with Jack?'

Cassie laughs. 'No, not really! It was sort of a one-time thing. Or maybe a two-time thing. I mean, we went out a couple of times and it was fine, but it's not like we had a connection or chemistry or anything. Not like you and Cal.'

I feel a little bit strange with this new information. I had assumed that Cassie and Jack were still merrily seeing each other and I just hadn't wanted to ask too much about it.

'Oh . . . yeah, I guess I am,' I say. Even though I don't really know how I feel about the whole situation, I do feel very protective of Cal, who is indisputably wonderful and who I am lucky to know, let alone date. 'It seems to be going well.'

'I guess I thought Cal would have mentioned that we fizzled out, seeing as he sees Jack pretty constantly!'

'Yeah, he's not . . . gossipy, like that, I guess?'

'Well, you two have probably got better things to talk about. Speaking of which: you've slept together now, right?' Cassie asks. I nod, wordlessly, hoping that's enough. 'How was it?'

'Yeah, it wasn't, like, bad or anything.'

'But . . . was it *good*?'

'Yes!' I say, defensively, as if it's ridiculous for her to even ask. 'It was really good. Cal's . . . talented,' I say. As an uncomfortable expression instantly clouds Cassie's face, I'm hit with the horrible realization that I'm *trying* to make her jealous. What the hell?!

'Well, I'm glad to hear that,' she says, looking out to the sea. She doesn't ask anything more about it, which I'm relieved about. 'Oh!' Cassie rummages in her bag and produces a brightly coloured card from between the pages of her book. 'You said it was Michael and Mark's anniversary, so I whipped up this little card.'

'They'll be delighted! You're too cute, honestly. Thanks, Cassie.'

Cassie pauses for a second, opens her mouth, closes it again. 'Are you feeling OK?' she asks, finally. 'Like, in general?'

'Yeah, why?' I ask too quickly. 'Feeling OK about what?'

'Um . . . I don't know, really. I just thought maybe you seemed stressed about something, or distracted, I guess. Like beyond what's going on with Daisy. Like . . . if I was gonna draw you right now I would draw you with this little swarm of bees buzzing around your head.' When I don't answer, she continues, 'You're my best friend. I wouldn't be very good at all this if I didn't notice when you seem different. When you seem kind of unhappy.'

I swallow down all the things that are still too confusing and difficult to even begin to unpick. I think about telling her the real story with Daisy, the fact that I kept the whole Cal thing from her, but I realize I don't like talking to Cassie about Cal. I want to keep them separate. 'I guess I'm stressed about next year, you know? The unknown.'

'Will you miss me?' Cassie asks, playfully.

'Are you serious?' I say, taken aback. 'A lot. An unhealthy amount.'

'I'm not going anywhere, it's not like we're dying.'

'I know that . . . it's just a long way.'

'And besides, you're the one who's leaving. That's always easier,' she says, looking down at her manicured hand resting on the picnic blanket.

'Easier than what?' I ask.

'Being the one who stays behind.' She wrinkles her nose but doesn't look at me. 'You've got a whole life to build. Mine will look pretty much the same.'

'You'll probably go to uni the next year, after you've done your art foundation course though, right? Like that's why you're doing it?'

She sighs. 'Yeah, I know that, but it feels a long way off. I'm kind of jealous of you getting to have an adventure now while I have to wait here for my life to begin. And without you, while you're having fun and going out with loads of new people in a new place. And forgetting about me . . .'

I don't know what to say to her. I want to tell her that

going to university feels like a huge mistake, like I'm just not ready for it, like I don't want to go and leave the only place I've ever lived and leave my best friend who I love so much. But I don't know how to say that without saying it directly, because saying it out loud would mean that I would have to do something about it or act on it and it's all too far down the road for that now. My only hope is that results day is a massive disaster! But I don't want her to think that I'm just skipping merrily off into the sunset to start a new life hundreds of miles away with loads of new people and that I'm going to forget about her. I could never, ever forget about her.

'I don't think it'll be that fun,' I say, quietly.

'Come on! You don't need to make me feel better about it! It's fine, really. I just wanted you to know I'll really miss you when you're gone. That's all,' she says, but she looks scared, like she knows she came close to unearthing something I didn't want her to. She looks at me quietly for a moment, as if expecting me to unburden myself to her. But I don't.

I want to. And not just about university and the future. I want to talk to her about myself. I want to explain myself to her, and show her all the things that I don't really understand. I want to show her who I am and ask if that's OK with her. I want to take all the little fragments of my feelings and see if she can help me put them together. I want to be assured of who I am but also feel vulnerable enough to leave room for the nerves and the excitement. And I don't want to do that with anyone else.

Ever since I met her, everything has felt a bit more right. A bit more like I'm at home. Every time I see her, I want to know when I'm seeing her again. A breeze has started along the beach, whipping the sand up in places, and I turn my head away from her and towards the direction of the wind and let it blow in my face. Because here and now, on this beach, on this Sunday, under this sky, I can finally see it. The truth.

I breathe in with shallow breaths as I realize the thing I've been avoiding all this time, the truth that I've been refusing to confront. I love Cassie. I love her in a way that's different to friendship. I love her and I'm in love with her and it's crept up on me in the past two years and I should have felt it coming and I didn't. I feel like a mosquito suspended in amber, something frozen in time, all my thoughts swirling around my head, finally understanding everything, finally understanding the meaning of things people had said to me, assumptions people had made. The pain that other people could see before I could. The fear that Cassie can see it too.

'Hey,' she says, putting her arm around me, which

177

makes me jump in surprise and then shrink in fear. 'Are you alright?'

I turn back to her, not wanting to cry. 'Yeah. I'm alright.' A real new thing. Acknowledging that I'm in love with Cassie.

On the bus back to Weston Bay, I lean my head against the grimy glass, close my eyes and just sit and think. For the first time I let myself look the whole situation in the face. It makes me feel tired, the idea of having to do something about it. The pressure of living differently. But it's all academic, because the one thing I would never want to do is compromise my friendship with Cassie.

To tell her how I feel and be rejected . . . to have her know that I love her and never be able to unsay it . . . it would pollute every interaction we ever have from now on. Unthinkable. I can't lose her. Not to time, not to distance, not to a guy, not to anything. And what about Cal? How can I feel so attracted to him if I know how I feel about Cassie?

I get off the bus a stop later than I usually would and walk round to Uncle Michael and Mark's house. We're having a highly informal tea and cake round at theirs to celebrate their wedding anniversary. We all mutually agreed it was – gasp – too hot for a roast, so we figured cake on a Saturday is just as good as roast on Sunday. As well as keeping up appearances for my whole family, I've also got the Daisy situation to contend with. I would very much rather curl up in a ball and fall asleep. Focus on getting through tea first. Then figure out how to bury the fact that I'm completely in love with my best friend in the whole wide world, who almost definitely doesn't feel the same way about me.

Gran answers the door. 'Good timing, Lil – I just made a chocolate cake with that chocolate buttercream filling you like. It was funny using someone else's kitchen, but I did my best . . .'

'Hi, Gran,' I say, but she's already halfway to the kitchen to retrieve the cake.

'Hello, baby!' Mum trills from the living room.

When I enter, Uncle Michael and Mark are side by side on the sofa, holding hands and watching a quiz show on TV. 'Alright, Lily?' they say simultaneously, standing to greet me. I feel sad to disturb the serenity of the moment with my presence. They look so uncomplicatedly happy. It melts me a bit.

'Happy anniversary!' I say, enveloping them in a group hug. 'I can't believe you've been married for *four years,* isn't that mad?'

'It honestly feels like it was yesterday,' Uncle Michael says, sitting back down on the sofa.

'You and Daisy in those sweet matching yellow dresses.'

Mark closes his eyes in delight and clutches his chest.

'We were thirteen! A decidedly un-cute age.'

'No!' Michael protests. 'You two are always the sweetest little things, however old you are.'

'Aren't you, Dais?' Mark nudges Daisy who's emerged from the kitchen with a tray full of cups and little slices of perfect chocolate sponge.

'Oh, hi, Lily. I didn't know you were here,' she says coldly, setting the china down on the coffee table before returning to the kitchen. Michael and Mark frown at Mum in the armchair and then look at me for an explanation, but I just shrug as if it's a mystery to me. I instantly hate myself for the betrayal but I'm not going to make tonight all about me and Daisy.

We eat our cake and watch the quiz show, Mark shouting answers between mouthfuls. 'Vanuatu!' and 'Jeremy Bentham!' and 'Beryllium!'

'Where do you store all this information?' Uncle Michael marvels, shaking his head at Mark.

'Aren't you glad you married a genius?'

'Even if you weren't a genius I would still be glad I married you, because you're so bloody kind,' he says, kissing him on the side of the head.

'Anyone would have been a step up from Jason, though,' Mum says, rolling her eyes. 'He was a right old whiner.'

'And he was so rude to that waiter that time we all went for dinner up in London, don't you remember, Luce?' Gran turns to Mum for back-up.

'Course I remember! Acting like it was his fault they were out of pheasant or whatever random meat he wanted. Awful man.'

'I was young! He was rich!' Michael wails.

'You weren't *that* young,' Gran scoffs.

'Yeah, you were literally in your *thirties*,' Mum says, reaching across from her armchair and poking her brother in the arm.

Mark is clearly loving it. 'Well, thank god I sat next to you on the night bus home from Pride all those years ago, is all I'm saying.'

The mention of Pride brings the homophobic posters crashing into my brain. And with it comes the realization that they are also targeting . . . me. First I was outraged on behalf of all the LGBTQIA+ people in my town. And now I guess I'm one of them. The thought leaves me with my forkful of cake suspended in mid-air, my mouth open, sat on the shaggy carpet rug beside Daisy. I sense Daisy's eyes on me, but when I look at her, she averts her gaze.

'Oh!' I remember Cassie's card. I retrieve it from my bag where I've stored it in the back cover of a book so it didn't get bent. 'This is from Cassie,' I say, handing it over to my uncle. He brushes the crumbs off his hands and takes it from me. He opens it and shows it to Mark. It's handmade, bold and graphic pieces of cut-out paper spelling HAPPY ANNIVERSARY in vivid, blocky writing. She has a way of making everything look cool and modern and unstudied, from her clothes to her cards.

'What a great girl she is. It's so sweet of her to think of us,' Uncle Michael says warmly, getting up from the sofa to put the card on the mantelpiece.

As if he knows that Cassie and dating are related, Mark asks Mum, 'How's your dating life going, Luce?'

Mum blushes. 'Well . . .'

'Well what?!' Michael demands, enthused.

'I was going to ask you two,' she says, turning her head to where Daisy and I are sitting side by side. 'If you wouldn't mind staying in tomorrow night. I've asked him round for dinner.'

'Bloody hell, you sly dog!' Michael shakes his head in mock disapproval.

'Who is this man? Is he the one from the . . . app?' Gran ventures, trying out her recently acquired technological knowledge.

'Actually yes,' Mum says quietly. 'His name is Tony and he's very nice and that's all I'll say on the matter.'

'Well, I'll be there,' Daisy says. 'Who knows if Lily

can make time in her busy schedule.'

'You don't need to worry about me, Daisy,' I say, sickly sweet, almost glad of the stupid distraction from what's going on in my head. 'You know I've always got time for the fair and equal pursuit of love.'

'Thanks girls,' says Mum, swallowing the last of her cake and choosing to ignore whatever's going on between us.

I look at Cassie's card on the mantelpiece and am filled with pride at knowing her. At the thought that she chose me to be her best friend. I shouldn't want to disrupt that. I don't want to disrupt that. I won't disrupt that.


Once we get home Mum settles in to do some reading in the living room, Crystal perched around her neck like a scarf. I'm about to join them when Daisy pads into the room and sits next to Mum. Instinctively, my body tenses. I don't really know how to behave around her. I start to head towards the door.

'So you girls are OK to meet Tony? I know it's soon, but I guess I just don't want to get too invested in him if you two think he's no good,' Mum says, halting my escape.

'That's a lot of responsibility,' I say.

'It's not that,' she says. 'It's just that I think you're good judges of character. And you're the most important people in my life.'

'Well, it'll be an honour to judge his character,' I say, plucking up the courage to look directly at Daisy, who nods in assent. One thing that can guarantee our cooperation: Mum. I stretch out my arms so Crystal disembarks from around my mum's neck and comes to me.

'We were always seeing each other tomorrow night, but I asked if he wanted to come here rather than us driving out to that pub with the fancy restaurant in it, you know the one . . .' Mum says, casting about for the name. 'He seemed a bit wary at first, I guess because it *is* quite soon.'

'You gotta do what you gotta do,' I say decisively.

'I hope you like him.'

'Same,' I say, stroking Crystal's fluffy tail.

'Oh! There was something else I wanted to talk to you girls about.'

'Uh-oh,' I say.

'It's about Crystal.'

'Oh my god, what's wrong?' Daisy gasps.

'Nothing's wrong – as you can see she's in perfect health. We've done a really good job of looking after her.'

'So?' Daisy urges.

'It's time for Crystal to go back to her real home,' says Mum. 'I didn't want to say too much at the time, but Crystal came from a woman who had been bringing her in for a while, whose husband was . . .' She clears her throat and touches her nose – a familiar nervous tic. 'Abusive. Violent. She wanted to leave him but didn't want to leave Crystal with him, and she knew she would find it hard to get somewhere to live if she had a cat with her. So I said I would look after her until things were more stable. That's why she's not allowed outside – we didn't want her to find her way home or for him to see her on the street.'

I feel a lump in my throat. For Crystal, and for her owner, and for my mum.

'So she's found somewhere to live?'

'Yes, she's got a place now, in another town, where some of her family live, and she can have Crystal back.'

We don't say anything for a moment. Crystal leaps down off my lap and curls up between my mum and Daisy.

'I've got to wrestle her into her carrier on Monday and drive her to a service station down the motorway after I'm finished at the surgery.'

'We'll miss you, Crystal,' I say. Daisy strokes her in her little dip in the sofa where the two cushions meet.

'She'll miss you, too,' Mum says.

I retreat to my room. I'm itching to paint. I get out my acrylics and put some old newspaper down on the floor so I don't wreck the carpet. My art teacher used to put on classical music while the A level students were working because she thought it would calm and inspire us, so I find a classical music playlist and flick through all of the tracks until I find one that I recognize and makes me feel at home. I settle on Bach's Cello Suite No. 1 and start putting lines on the page, building the structure and fleshing out the outline and softening it. I try not to think so hard, and add depth and shadow, making it more real and making it perfect and making it human. Making it Cassie. The person who's always on my mind.

I've always said I don't like to paint or draw people because I think it'll reveal something about me on the page. Maybe this is the thing I've been scared of revealing, even to myself.

I'm in love with Cassie. I'm in love with Cassie. And I've always been in love with Cassie. Cal is wonderful in so many ways and I'm so attracted to him. But he's not her. She's all there is.

Does this mean I'm gay? I mean . . . it can't, right? I fancy Cal. I fancy Cal a lot. But that just doesn't eclipse what feel for Cassie. It's like it's all those feelings can be happening at the same time, but it's what I feel for Cassie that burns brightest. I guess that means I'm . . . bi. I'm bi. I am bisexual. That's me. That's the answer.

It's Cal I should be friends with and Cassie I should be in a relationship with – I've had it the wrong way round the whole time.

# CHAPTER ELEVEN

At Cal's the next day, I am paralysed by guilt. I am crushingly aware that it's wrong of me to keep seeing him, knowing how I feel about Cassie. But something keeps me there and keeps me silent. I like being in his company. It feels comfortable, and we have fun together, and it's a place where I don't have to think too much.

We watch a film on his laptop and drink some fancy beer he bought at a fancy craft beer place in town. We have sex again, and it's great, but I just can't keep my brain engaged. But amid all my fears and anxieties, Cal doesn't make me panic.

'I can't believe the weekend is almost over,' I say as I'm getting dressed again.

'Check you out with your stable ice-cream salesperson lifestyle! Weekends don't mean a thing when you work shifts.'

'Ha! Yeah, I guess, I hadn't thought of that.'

'What did you get up to yesterday?' Cal asks.

'I went for a picnic with Cassie on the beach in Seaforth,' I say, but as soon as I say it I wonder if it's setting off some kind of alarm bells in him, like her name suddenly sounds different in my mouth. So I continue, 'Then stopped off to see my uncle and his husband – the ones who run the Lighthouse – it was their anniversary.' I fasten my bra and wiggle it into place.

'Fun, at least more fun than a Saturday in the school holidays!'

'Sorry I can't stick around,' I say, ruefully.

'No, it's totally fine, it's a big night! I hope Tony's a good guy.'

'Same. At least it's a good entry for my Summer of New Things: meet a man my mum is dating.'

'Look, if you ever need more inspo for your new things, just ask. It's a cute project!'

'Here's one: do you want to do something tomorrow?' I ask. I feel like it's not good for me to spend too much time with Cassie right now. And given I can't hang out with Daisy these days . . .

'Wow! That doesn't sound like you!' Cal laughs good-naturedly, pulling his T-shirt on over his head. 'Asking me out . . . truly a new thing!'

'Sorry about that,' I say with a blush. 'That's why I'm doing this whole project . . .'

'Look, it's fine. And I'm working tomorrow night but could do Tuesday?'

'Let's do Tuesday, then.'

The knowledge that at the end of the summer we'll go our separate ways is making everything feel a bit easier, a bit less high-risk. And it's not like I don't enjoy hanging out with him. And I don't *not* enjoy sleeping with him. It's all just floating along on a limited timeline. And besides, it's easier to deal with being with him because I *don't* have all the feelings I have for Cassie: the thorny, uncomfortable, difficult feelings that feel like they're going to suffocate me and wrap me up in a cosy blanket at the same time.

On the way home, trying to convince myself everything is still just fine and normal, I text Cassie about meeting Mum's new man tonight. Even writing a text has become impossible: I write and rewrite it, just to make extra sure it sounds like nothing's changed.

What starts as:

> Hey you! Huge news, meeting Mum's internet bf today, hope he's good enough for her. How are you / what are you up to / can't wait to see you tomorrow for another day of TOIL AND FUN xx

Becomes:

Huge news, meeting Mum's internet
bf today, hope he's good enough for her.
Will tell you about it tomorrow either way.

Am I going to have to live like this forever now?

When I get home, the house smells amazing, a chicken roasting in the oven and Mum looking like a slightly more groomed version of her usual beautiful self.

'Thank god you're here!' she exclaims. 'I thought you forgot. Having too much fun with your own mystery man, I assume.'

'As if! I've got to meet this guy so I can report back to Uncle Michael about whether he's any good for you,' I say with a naughty grin. She swats me with a towel.

I run upstairs to shower and change. I can hear Daisy in her room. I don't think things will go back to normal until we talk everything through properly. And there's no sign of that happening any time soon. So I may have to actually do something about this. At least for tonight. Once I'm dressed, I present myself in Daisy's room whether she wants me to or not. We have to create a united front in support of Mum tonight.

'Look, I accept there's still . . .' I gesture messily between us from the doorframe. 'Whatever's going on here. But we can't make it weird for Mum. Right?'

Daisy sighs languidly. 'Right.'

I breathe a sigh of relief. 'So,' I say, sliding onto her bed while she pulls a T-shirt on in front of the mirror. 'What do you think this guy will be like? Good? Awful? Hideous?'

'Honestly, I have no idea. It's not like we have anything to compare him to, either. We have no track record to judge him by, or to predict what he'll be like. This is a whole new world.'

'It's true,' I say. God it feels good just to talk to her again. 'Well, fingers crossed he's the love of her life.'

'Shall we go downstairs and loiter in the living room?' she proposes.

'Alright,' I say, and follow her down to the sofa where we sit side by side, identical twins but completely different. It doesn't take long for a figure to advance down the front path and ring the doorbell.

'Mum, your gentleman caller's here!' I yell to her in the kitchen.

'Keep your voice down, you little maniac!' Mum says as she dashes past the living room to open the front door, her long, fair hair swinging behind her like a sail.

I hear them exchange greetings, and it sounds relaxed even though meeting the family is a bold new frontier in any relationship. Daisy and I look at each other awkwardly, unsure if we're meant to wait here or go out there to say hello, so we just wait on the sofa in a kind of uncomfortable forward-lean in case we're called upon to get up. We listen, holding our breath, as Mum and the man exchange pleasantries in the hall, and it takes so long that we burst into a nervous giggle. Our first shared laugh for a long time. Finally they appear in the living room, so I spring to my feet to say hello to— Señor Mango Sorbet?! I instinctively reach into my pocket for my phone before remembering, firstly, that it's upstairs, and secondly, it would be incredibly rude of me to text Cassie before I've even uttered a word to him.

'Hi, I'm Tony, nice to . . .' He trails off as he looks me in the face. The very profoundly, deeply unimpressed face. I can tell he's turning it all over in his mind, the click of recognition, but from where?

And that's when it all falls into place for me. His not-very-visible profile photo. His wife saying he hadn't been around much recently. He's just a sad man who's cheating on his wife, and of all the women in the world, he had to be cheating on his wife with my mum. What a way to kick off her online dating career.

'Hello, Tony. I'm Lily,' I say, evenly. 'Nice to meet you.' I see the penny drop; he knows exactly where he's seen me before and he knows that I've seen him there too, and he knows, most of all, that I know he's very much married.

'Does anyone want a drink? Tony, what can I get you?' my mum interjects, fortunately oblivious to the tension.

'Uhhh . . .' He snaps out of his trance. 'Can I have a beer, please?'

'Any preference?'

'No, I'll drink anything,' he says, smiling weakly.

And with that, my mum leaves the living room, and Daisy and I sit on the sofa while Tony (assuming that even is his real name, at this point, who knows?) goes to sit on the armchair where Crystal is stretched out on the top.

'She won't bite,' Daisy says warmly when she sees him looking wary.

'She means the cat,' I say, drily.

'Ha!' Tony says, looking at me nervously, like I'm a ticking time bomb.

We don't have long until Mum reappears with his drink and says, 'Your timing was spot on – it's all ready now, actually, if you want to come through?' She seems a little nervous, which is understandable. It's not just the nerves of a new guy, but also the nerves of this being the first new guy in . . . well, a really long time. And in no time at all, this is all going to fall apart for her.

We shuffle into the kitchen and sit around the small dining table. It's weird to have four people sitting at it rather than our usual three. Mum elegantly carves the chicken and drizzles some sauce over the little pyramid of string beans already on the plate.

'This looks wonderful, Lucy,' Tony says, tugging at the collar of his shirt. As he does, I notice the tiny dent in his finger where his wedding ring would usually be.

'Thank you,' Mum says, a light blush appearing on her cheeks.

'So,' Tony says. He looks up from his plate. 'Are you two girls going to become vets like your mum?'

'No chance,' says Daisy. 'Too much interaction with bodily fluids for my liking.'

'Yes, that is a rather important piece of the puzzle, one's tolerance for things too indelicate to bring up over dinner,' Mum says pointedly.

'And what do you do, Tony?' I ask. I'd hoped it would come out politely inquisitive but I fear from the look on my mum and sister's faces that it sounded more like a challenge.

'I . . . well, I'm a management consultant.'

'And what does that mean?'

'It means advising companies on how to do their work better for less money.'

'So firing people?'

'Lily!'

'No, no, it's alright . . . yes, sometimes it means that,

but most of the time it's just how to cut costs around the business.'

'And you're doing your consulting for a company based in Weston Bay? Is that right?' I ask, cutting up some string beans and dragging them through the creamy, buttery sauce on my plate.

'At the moment, yes,' Tony says, and I'm sure I can see beads of sweat forming on his brow. He's really not bad-looking: grey-black hair, tanned skin, big brown eyes, nice clothes. Probably chosen for him by his wife. I wonder what she's up to tonight. 'The Mrs', he called her. I wonder if he even is a management consultant or if that's a convenient explanation for why he's not available all the time and why he would be staying in a hotel.

I don't say anything. Instead I smile sweetly and let someone else take over the conversation. I disappear into my thoughts, wondering what to do about the whole thing. Cassie stuff, uni anxiety, Cal guilt, it's all feeling like a mountain on top of me. And now this! Having to figure out what to do about *this*. My chest feels tight.

'Lily?' Mum says, making me realize I haven't been concentrating for a while now.

'Huh?' I reply.

'Tony was asking what your plans are for next year,' she prompts.

'Oh, uh,' I swallow. 'An art history degree at Leeds.'

'Wow,' he says, smiling. 'That sounds great. It'll be good to have a change of scenery, a whole new start, won't it?'

'Yes,' I say, although even I know I sound unconvinced. 'That's what I keep hearing.'

'Art history, that sounds fun,' he continues.

'I hope so,' I say. 'I'm not sure if it's the right thing for me, but I'm willing to find out.'

Before he can reply, my mum cuts in, frowning, her knife and fork poised to cut but now suspended. 'What do you mean, not sure if it's the right thing?' I instantly know I shouldn't have said anything.

'Oh, no, nothing,' I say quickly, shooting a glance to Daisy so she doesn't unburden herself about my anxieties. 'I just mean that maybe I would be better off focusing on painting, rather than theory, but I'm not going to change my mind now.'

'OK . . .' Mum says, looking a bit baffled and sceptical but aware that now isn't the time, not while her new man is in the building. Even if her new man is a lying bastard. But I guess she doesn't know that yet.

'How about you, Daisy?' Tony asks.

'Daisy's a science genius,' I say, infused with a Rose family solidarity that supersedes our fight. And also in pursuit of some much-needed brownie points in preparation for when I expose Tony as a bad egg. 'She's going to do physics and probably change the world.'

'Science isn't the only way to change the world,' says my mum. 'I'm pretty sure art can do that, too.'

'I guess,' I say, shrugging. It's hard to focus on the here and now when my brain is overloaded with the stress of knowing that Mum is an unwilling accessory to adultery. Part of me hopes I'm wrong, that I've misunderstood or misremembered something. But I know I haven't.

When we've finished the chicken, Daisy goes to use the bathroom while Mum is sorting out dessert. Tony and I sit in silence, glaring at each other across the table, almost daring the other to speak. I wait a moment before dashing upstairs, pretending I need my phone which I left in my bedroom. I stand on the stairs, biding my time, and then grab Daisy by the wrist as she emerges from the bathroom.

'Ow!' Daisy looks down at my hand and then up at my face. 'What are you doing? And why are you being so weird this evening?'

'I need to talk to you,' I whisper. 'Quietly.'

'Ugh, what drama have you got going on now?' Daisy asks dismissively.

'It's not about me,' I say through gritted teeth. 'Come on.' I drag her back up to the bathroom and lock us in where we won't be disturbed, at least for a few minutes.

I put the lid down on the toilet and sit on top of the seat. She sits on the edge of the bath, resting her hands on either side of her and stretching her legs out in front.

'So?'

'Have you noticed a certain *tension* between Tony and me?' I ask, to see if it's something our mum would have noticed too, or if I've been able to keep a lid on it.

'Eurgh, gross, you haven't been on a date with him as well, have you?' Daisy asks, wrinkling her nose in disgust.

I roll my eyes at her. Now is not the time. 'I don't mean sexual tension, you absolute fool.'

'Well, no, either way, I hadn't noticed anything.'

'OK, good, that's good,' I say.

'Again I ask you . . . so?' Daisy says impatiently. 'What's the big problem? Why are we in here?' She gestures wildly around at the bathroom.

'The big problem is that Mum's new man is very much married!'

'No!' Daisy says. 'Are you sure? Like actually, really sure?'

'Yes, I am *really* sure.'

'You promise you're not just making a fuss over nothing? She doesn't need that right now.'

'Oh my god, Daisy, I know that! I'm not trying to cause

trouble! Of course I'm sure, I serve him most days at the ice-cream stand *with his wife*!'

'Are you sure it's him? The same guy?'

'Yes I'm sure! He's such a regular that we even have a nickname for him – he's Señor Mango Sorbet!'

'Well . . .' Daisy shrugs, casting about for other options. 'Maybe it's not his wife?'

'It is his wife! He literally referred to her as 'the Mrs'! That's pretty unambiguous.'

'Oh, damn . . .'

'And besides, he is being weird. He knows I know! When we go back downstairs, just look at his finger where his wedding ring should be. It's got a little dent in it, you can *see* he usually wears a ring.'

'This is so bad . . . I feel terrible for Mum already and she doesn't even know . . .' Daisy bites her lip.

'We'll get round to that later. I just had to tell someone so I didn't go completely mad.'

'Maybe she does know and doesn't care?' Daisy, with her rational, scientific mind, *must* be rattled if she's coming up with a suggestion like that.

'Come on, does that sound like Mum? Based on everything you know about her?'

'Not really . . .' Daisy mumbles. 'No.'

'No,' I repeat emphatically. 'This isn't what she wants.'

*

We don't make our mind up about anything, but having told Daisy makes me feel better about the whole situation. I guess that's what sisters are for. There it is, a little pang of regret at feeling distant from Daisy at a time when we need each other most. When we go back downstairs, it's obvious that Mum and Tony were just making out, which is disgusting in its own right, not to mention an evident lack of remorse on Tony's part about being a cheating scumbag. I'm not sorry when it's time for him to go – fortunately there's no discussion of him staying over. I bet he's mad as hell about that, squandering his one evening a week of philandering.

'So . . .' Mum says, once he's left. 'What did you think?!'

Daisy sighs and for a second I wonder if she's going to tell her. 'It doesn't matter what we think! It's you who's going out with him!'

'I know that.' She bats away the idea. 'But it's important to me what you two think! You have good instincts about people. That's one of the reasons I wanted him to come round. I trust your judgement.'

'Well . . .' I say, biting my thumbnail. 'He seems OK, I guess.'

'You don't sound too enthusiastic . . .'

'It's not that,' says Daisy. 'I think we just need to get to know him better.' That seems to satisfy Mum.

In bed later that evening, just as I'm about to turn out the light, I hear a soft knock on the door.

'Come in,' I whisper, and Daisy enters in her pink summer pyjamas. She comes and sits on my bed.

'What are we gonna do about Mum?'

I sigh. 'I don't know . . . do you think we should tell her?'

Daisy looks at me out of the corner of her eye. 'So now you're anti-secrets?'

I choose to ignore that. 'I'm worried she's going to hate me for ruining everything if I do say something. I wish I didn't know that guy, then none of this would be the big moral conundrum that it's turned out to be.'

'It's not a great way to begin her dating life, is it?'

'Good to know you care about that when it's not to do with me,' I say sharply. 'But no, it's not. I don't understand why it's so hard to just meet someone good and kind who's crazy about you and you're crazy about them and you can just enjoy the whole thing without all this drama.'

Daisy's quiet for a second, looking slightly confused. 'But you have that, right?'

'What?'

'You have that, with Cal, I mean.' I'm taken aback by her sudden sincerity. I almost don't know what to do with it.

'Uh, yeah,' I say instinctively, without wanting to linger too long on the thought. My phone vibrates and I see a text from Cassie, asking how tonight went. Where to start! 'But back to Mum.'

'Are you going to tell her?'

A thought occurs to me. 'He comes to the stand most days. If he does show his face tomorrow, I'll tell him he has to end it with Mum. Although I guess I can't really do that if Lady Red Plum is around . . .'

'Who is Lady Red Plum?!'

'Oh, sorry, I mean his wife.'

'You're so weird . . .' Daisy mutters drily, but she can't help chuckling.

'If he doesn't show up, with or without her, I guess I'll have to tell Mum myself.'

'Urgh, I hate this,' Daisy says, shaking her head and getting up to leave.

'Same,' I say.

'What's that?' Daisy asks.

'What's what?'

'That,' she says, pointing at the windowsill where my painting of Cassie rests against the glass, waiting for a purpose. I keep thinking about getting rid of it but something stops me. I instantly feel mortified that Daisy has seen it, like an X-ray of my insides. Just a portrait of Cassie, done in acrylics. Simple, face-on, from the shoulders up, wearing that vibrant purple lipstick that only looks good on her, a cream scarf with red polka dots tied in her hair like it was the first time we hung out after college. It is, unmistakeably, her. It captures her big, brown eyes. The glinting gold of her nose ring. Her apple cheeks, her dimples. There is no need to change her features or flatter her. She is perfect just the way she is.

'. . . nothing.' I answer, avoiding her eyes.

'Not to inflate your ego but . . . it's beautiful.'

# CHAPTER TWELVE

I'm lying awake on Monday morning, trying not to think about Señor Mango Sorbet, or Cal, or Cassie (who I forgot to text back last night amid the drama), or uni, or how mixed up I feel about, well, everything. It's a good job I needed to wake up a bit earlier than usual today anyway, so I can have some time with Crystal before she returns to her real mum. I'm not surprised when I pad into the living room that Daisy is already there, stroking Crystal on her lap.

'She's a good cat, isn't she?'

'Yeah,' I say. 'It's no wonder her owner wouldn't want to be without her.' Crystal has jumped off Daisy's lap and come to slink through my legs. I pick her up and hold her like a baby, kissing her on her fluffy head. 'I'll miss you, Crystal.'

I carry her back to the sofa and sit next to Daisy, and Crystal stretches out across our laps. We sit in silence and stroke her.

'You two can be so cute sometimes,' Mum says when she comes in, holding a cup of tea.

'Alas, I can't stay here forever, I can't leave Cassie hanging,' I say, standing up while seamlessly trying to transfer Crystal to Daisy's arms. 'Crystal, you are a perfect cat, and I am so happy for you that you're going to see your mum again.'

I feel a little sad when I'm getting dressed, but I know it's for the best. I wish Mum didn't have this on her plate after work as well as whatever the Tony situation's going to throw at her. When I head out, I blow a kiss to Crystal, and hug Mum, which is something I should do more often. In the few seconds I have my arms around her, I'm flooded with so many thoughts and questions. How would she feel if she knew about me? I don't even know why I'm wondering about this, I *know* she would be fine about it, she wouldn't even think twice. But I wonder if it'll change how she sees me.

Actually, getting dressed for work is a new challenge in itself. I wonder what I should wear for my first shift since . . . well, since I figured things out. I feel like I'm looking at everything through new eyes, and with this fresh perspective I feel a not-so-strange motivation to look cute for work. Not just a T-shirt and jeans anymore. I throw on a short-sleeve shirt dress with bright brushstroke prints all over it. Cuter than usual.

'Oh boy,' I say to Cassie when I get to the stand. I try to

pretend my heart isn't racing and my mouth isn't dry and that I feel totally fine seeing her. Her smile is dazzling. I just need to keep pretending everything's normal. Fortunately I have a good conversational distraction. 'What a time I have had since I last saw you!'

'How?! It was only two days ago?' Cassie's wearing navy-blue lipstick and a gold lamé jumpsuit underneath her apron and looks, frankly, incredible. 'You look cute, by the way!'

'Well,' I begin, trying not to take that compliment to heart and trying not to look too closely at her eyelashes even though the sun is adding a soft shine to their inky black lengths. 'It concerns last night's cosy little get-together with Mum's man. So he came over for dinner last night as you know, and it was none other than . . .'

'Who?!' Cassie says, no patience for my dramatic flourish.

'Señor Mango Sorbet! Whose name is actually Tony, which is much less interesting.'

'Wow . . . he's, like, definitely married isn't he?' Cassie grimaces.

'Definitely.'

'Did you tell your mum?'

'Not yet, I've decided if he comes by the stand today I'll tell him to end it, and if he doesn't do it himself, I'll have to.'

'Bloody hell,' she says, wide-eyed. 'I hope I'm not off for a loo break if he does show up! I want to see you, you know, *getting involved* with something. Most unlike you.'

'Really?' I ask, defensively.

She pauses like she's trying to figure out the kindest way to say what she wants to. 'You are the best person in the world but you are not a *doer,* by nature. You are totally capable of taking action, but you have to feel like it's something only you can do. You have more power and agency than you realize, I think.'

'Huh. Well. Today's new thing can be sorting something out myself for once. If he shows up.'

'Speak of the devil,' she says, and I whip round to see him approaching the stand, solo. 'Oh my god, what a way to begin our working week!' Cassie's breathing heavily, electrified with the impending drama. She reaches out and grabs my hand to squeeze it but I yank it away like I've been burned.

Cassie doesn't have time to react because Tony's walking quickly, approaching the stand and looking over his shoulder every few steps.

'Hello, Tony,' I say flatly.

'Look, can I have a word?' He tugs at his collar and I can see he's sweating even though the temperature is pleasantly bearable.

'Alright,' I say, pulling off my baseball cap and slinking out from behind the stand. 'I won't be long, Cassie.' She looks disappointed not to witness the exchange.

We walk in silence to the other side of the green. 'So?' I ask.

'Look,' he says again. 'I know what I've done is wrong, I know that.'

'Good. Do you want a medal?'

'No . . . I just wanted to say, it was stupid of me. I've never done anything like it before. I was just . . . bored. I didn't really plan on meeting anyone on the app, and then I started talking to your mum and she's just so . . . brilliant and beautiful and I was so bored at home.'

'I honestly don't care what your reasons are, all I care about is that you're going to stick a pin in this,' I say, looking him right in the eye.

'I will, I will, I'm sorry,' he grovels. 'But please, if you see my wife around town . . . I'm begging you not to say anything.'

I exhale furiously. 'She doesn't deserve this. And you don't deserve her. But I'm not going to get involved in someone else's family drama.'

'Thank you,' he says, looking like he's about to collapse with pure relief. 'Thank you so much. It's been a nightmare trying to juggle this . . . hotels, lies, feelings.'

'Don't try to get me to sympathize with you. You're a grown man. You've made your bed. Now I have to get back to work,' I say. 'Just let my mum down gently, she's a person too.'

'I will, I promise. I swear.'

'Alright. Bye, Tony. Hope you enjoy the rest of the summer without your mango sorbet.'

'Jesus, I hadn't even thought of that . . .' he says as he turns to walk back towards town.

I head back to the stand and recount the details to Cassie.

'God, what a snake!'

'Do you think I was wrong to agree not to tell his wife?'

'No, not at all. It's not your family. You've done your bit for *your* family.'

A family with four kids turns up at the stand in search of ice cream, all different flavours and configurations of cones and cups. I go to pick up the scoop but Cassie reaches for it at the same time and I'm just left holding her hand like an idiot. I look up at her and she's laughing and I realize I should laugh too, so I crack a smile and hope that's enough.

Having this stuff going on with my mum has been a convenient, if all too brief distraction from the fact that things aren't really working for me and Cal. But I don't want to throw it all away because I just *like* him so much. He's so good and kind and fun to spend time with and hang out and watch films with and, honestly? He's hot as hell and that counts for a lot! Plus, he's leaving at the end of the summer anyway. And as long as I'm with Cal it means there's no reason at all for me to think about Cassie as anything more than a friend. He's like the world's hottest safety net.

A few times throughout the day, I get the feeling Cassie wants to say something to me, but every time she opens her mouth to speak, she shuts it again and then comes out with casual chat a moment later. But nothing we talk about today is enough to stop my mind from wandering. I crave distraction. The word *homesick* keeps swirling around in my head. It sounds childish, not something an eighteen-year-old should be thinking about. But do we ever really outgrow our families? It's like all the unhappiness has started already and is piling up on top of me. I don't even get to enjoy *this* time I have left because all I can do is worry about the future.

I take a different route home than usual, wanting to drag it out a bit. It takes me past a bus shelter, and pasted on one of the walls I notice another one of those fascist posters. I tear it down, rip it in half and shove it in the bin next to the shelter, and I feel the anger bubbling inside me at the way Tony thought he could behave with brilliant, beautiful women. At the way Crystal's owner was driven out of her home by an abusive man. At the way people like my uncle and Mark and . . . well, me, have to be afraid on the streets of their town. At the way anyone would feel empowered enough in their own disgusting beliefs to put up something like this.

When I get home, I run upstairs, nearly knocking Daisy over in the process, and throw myself on my bed. I lie face down, buried in my pillow, and let myself cry and cry and turn everything over in my head and really let myself think about how much I don't want to go away to university next year and how much I don't want to stop painting and how much I don't want to leave Cassie. I lie there for a while with my face in the damp pillow, heaving with ragged breathing. Over my panicked sobs, I'm sure I can hear someone calling my name.

'Lily!' I realize it's my sister calling impatiently from the garden. At least this time I know she'll just want to find out if Tony showed up today, rather than yell at me about something I've done. 'Lily!' Actually, it sounds urgent, so I hoist myself out of bed and make my way downstairs, through the kitchen and out the back door. I take care not to let Crystal out before remembering Crystal is gone, and I try not to feel sad about it, instead remembering to feel happy that she's back with her real owner who probably missed her loads.

'What?' I ask, which comes out slightly impatiently.

'Look,' urges Daisy. And I see what it is that she wants me to look at. The little garden is absolutely full of painted lady butterflies. Some are beating their wings in the air, others are resting on the flowers in bloom. Their black-dappled red wings are glowing in the evening light, and the sight of them all together is just extraordinary. 'It's the buddleia, that's what's attracting them,' she says, pointing to the purple bush in one corner of the garden.

'It's amazing, Daisy. It's so beautiful,' I say, and I really mean it. 'You did this!'

'Nature did this, I just helped it all on its way.' She blushes.

'Well, it's really cool. Thank you,' I say, pulling gently on her long dark plait that's resting on the back of her old, oversized T-shirt. We stand in silence and watch the butterflies swirl and land and lift and fly away until one by one they're all gone. I feel my eyes fill with tears at all the time I've wasted this summer arguing with Daisy, at all the things she could have shown me, told me, taught me in that time, all the things I could have talked to her about. She turns to look at me and when she sees me, she almost looks hurt herself. Wow, my eyes must be pretty bloodshot.

'Are you OK?'

'Yes,' I say.

'Well, that's a lie.'

'No, I was not feeling great before, but I'm . . . a bit better now. Don't worry about me.'

She pauses for a second. 'Did he come to the stand today?'

'Yeah,' I say. 'And he didn't bring his wife with him this time. It was like he knew what we wanted him to do.' I give her a quick recap of what was said at Palmers'.

'I feel so bad for Mum, she seemed to really like him.'

'There are plenty more fish in the sea,' I say.

'You would say that.' Daisy rolls her eyes.

I choose to ignore her. I guess we're still not quite right yet. 'It's just rubbish timing, isn't it?'

'With Crystal going back? Yeah.'

And as if saying Crystal's name could summon Mum, we hear the front door close. We look at each other nervously and head inside.

Mum's flopped on the sofa, jacket and shoes still on, with Crystal's empty cat carrier next to her.

'What a day,' she says. 'What a day!'

'Are you alright?' Daisy asks, trying to sound neutral.

'Well, Tony's gone, for starters,' she says.

'Oh no!' I say, bracing myself. 'What happened?'

'He rang me up. He told me that actually, he was married, and that actually, he just joined the apps because he was bored, and actually wasn't expecting to like me so much and that actually, it's all my fault for being so damn charming.' She sounds more irritated than upset by it, like he's a mere inconvenience. 'Sometimes you try something new . . . you know,' she says, looking at me gently. 'And sometimes it works out and somctimes it doesn't. I guess it's the trying that's the important part. The feeling of letting yourself do something new, even if it feels scary. Even if it ends in a slightly unfortunate way . . .'

Suddenly the air is punctuated with a squeak.

'Oh my god, what was that?!' I ask, clasping my chest.

'Well,' says Mum, gently lifting up the cat carrier, which we can now see is not empty at all. But it's not Crystal. It's a tiny little version of Crystal, all white fur and bright blue eyes. 'The local cat shelter had kittens that they were struggling to rehome because there were just so many of them. So on my way back from meeting Crystal's mum at the service station, I thought I would relieve them of one.'

Daisy looks like she's going to cry. 'Mum, this is the best thing that's ever happened.'

'She can keep me company when you two are away,' Mum says, opening the carrier and letting the tiny white furball trot out. I gasp with unadulterated delight.

'I could die! It's so cute! Is it a girl or a boy?' I ask as the furball sits nervously just outside the cat carrier.

'She's a girl. Aoife at the shelter said they've been calling her Princess. I figured we've still got all the cat stuff from Crystal. Not that she's a replacement for Crystal. I just realized how nice it had been having her around.'

'I guess we can call her Princess,' Daisy says with a shrug, kneeling down on the floor to stroke her.

'She does look like a Princess,' I agree. I lower myself down to join them, looking into her enormous blue eyes, extending a finger to induce her to come to me. Daisy and I stay down there while Mum makes dinner and puts out kitten food for our new friend.

'Mum,' I ask as we're eating dinner and Princess is still cowering in the living room, 'can Cassie come round and meet Princess?'

She thinks for a moment. 'I don't see why not.'

Cassie's at ours an hour later, playing with this sweet, perfect baby. Princess is shy and nervous but not averse to being held, and even works up the courage to chase a ball that Cassie rolls away from her. Cassie's so gentle with her that it almost breaks my heart to watch them. I feel all soft and squishy inside. It's funny how a day can turn around, just like that. Or, it's funny how *someone* can turn your day around, just like that.

# CHAPTER THIRTEEN

By Friday, everything has calmed down. A bit. I'm trying to just . . . wait out my feelings for Cassie. Just riding it out until it's all over. Until I'm shipped off to Leeds, and I have to leave her behind. Only six more days until results day and all chances of escape are taken from me. I've realized that this is pretty much my default state: waiting. I'm a coward. I'm essentially in a relationship with someone because I'm too scared to properly confront the fact that I'm in love with my best friend. And it's not like I can just avoid her, or simply push everything to the side and enjoy my time with her. I'm with her every day at Palmer's Ices, and it's getting harder and harder to remember how to keep things light when I've got so much going on in my head, and the person I most want to talk to about all of it is part of the problem.

At least Mum doesn't seem too badly knocked by the whole Tony thing. Plus, last night I saw her swiping on an app again which can surely only be good news. Unless there's another cheating scumbag just around the corner, which I truly pray there is not. Not one I would recognize.

Princess is settling in nicely and has become less nervous around us. She also makes a very good selfie companion, especially when you put a ridiculous filter on her.

But I can't think about any of that now, because Cassie is right next to me on the stand, in another dazzling Cassie creation, being generally lovely and I'm just kind of standing here.

'What can we get you?' I perkily ask our latest customer.

The young man at the counter pushes his sunglasses onto his head, showcasing the huge tattoo of a rodeo horse on his forearm. He pensively scratches the stubble on his sharp jawline. 'Dark chocolate, I reckon.'

Even though I'm serving him, Cassie pipes up beside me, 'One scoop or two?' The silver scoop is already in her hand, ready to do his bidding.

He squints down at the change in his hand, then glances at the prices written on the inside of the glass. Back at the change in his hand. 'One. Thanks.'

But Cassie picks up a two-scoop cup. 'Oh, don't worry about it,' she says, getting to work. 'It's on me.'

The guy blushes as Cassie passes him the cup with a wink and he says, 'Cheers!'

As he walks away, he looks back over his shoulder and gives her an appreciative nod. Does she like him?

'What was that about?' I ask, trying to keep my tone

light but, obviously, failing.

'I thought his tattoos were cool, and then I felt bad because he clearly didn't have enough money.' She shrugs, looking at me in confusion. 'We never give anything away for free, I figured one little cup wouldn't hurt.'

'I guess . . .' I say quietly.

'What?' Cassie asks, looking me in the eyes, as if daring me to say something more.

'No, nothing.'

Great. Now I've caused weird vibes with Cassie because I can't just be normal. I can't even *act* normal. Half an hour later, after serving another flurry of customers, though fortunately this time without incident, my gaze is caught by Cassie fiddling with something in her hands. I try to catch a glimpse of it but she senses me looking and turns away. Fine. She can be like that if she wants to. I stare fixedly at the sea for a couple of minutes, neither of us saying anything. Finally, she turns to me, palm outstretched, on top of which sits a Palmer's Ices napkin contorted into the shape of a swan.

'A gift from me to you,' she says. 'I realized I was watching too much pointless shit on YouTube so decided to teach myself something useful for once.'

'I genuinely love and admire your perception of *useful*,' I say, beaming.

'You think it's cute? You think I'm talented?' Cassie asks, hopping from foot to foot.

'I think you're cute *and* talented,' I reply, before realizing that wasn't what she said at all. She stops hopping. We look at each other awkwardly, but I don't attempt to clarify what I meant. It would only make it worse. She adjusts her baseball cap and turns to serve our next customer.

Finally, when some of the knotty awkwardness from earlier has dissipated, we take our lunch in shifts. 'I made my mum stop the van on the way here this morning,' Cassie says to me from the nearby bench where she's eating her peanut butter bagel. Always crunchy, never smooth. 'I saw another one of those racist posters and had to take it down.'

'Ugh, I thought they were all gone.'

'It looked like it had been there a couple of weeks, so fingers crossed that's the last one.'

'I hope there aren't more to come . . .' And then I think to myself: you know what would be *really* out of my comfort zone? Doing something for once in my life rather than sitting back and being a passive observer of everything that's going on around me. I think of Cassie feeling unsafe in the town she comes to work in every day. I think of those men I heard spitting out bile about my sister and her friends.

It's like she's read my mind. Cassie nibbles her lip and

looks out to the glittering sea. 'I want to go one better. I want to make my own.'

'Your own?'

'My own posters. Tearing them down used to be good enough, but I've been thinking about it and I want to make my own. Let's call it a . . . public art project.' Her face looks focused, determined. I know nothing can stand in the way when Cassie sets her mind on something. And why should it, especially something like this?

'Do you want a hand?' I ask, half expecting her to say no.

She looks at me, as if sizing me up. 'Yeah, why not?'

'Do you want to come back to mine after work tonight? We can use all my art stuff to get it done. Plus my mum will leave us alone.'

She thinks for a moment. 'Hey, we spent two years working next to each other in the art room and we never did anything collaboratively. I guess that makes it . . . a new thing for you.'

'New thing! New thing! New thing!' we chant together, glad to have a sense of purpose.

'I love it when a plan comes together,' she says.

Almost as soon we step through the front door, I'm struck by a sick jolt of horror: the painting. My portrait of Cassie. So transparently the work of someone looking at their subject overwhelmed with love. And it's sitting right there on my windowsill.

'Just a minute!' I call down over my shoulder, leaving her standing in the hall as I run up the stairs, two at a time – no mean feat.

'What are you doing?!' Cassie yells back, bemused.

'It's a mess up here, just give me a second to throw some stuff in a cupboard!'

'This isn't the first time I've seen your room, you know . . . I know what you're like.' *I hope not*, I think to myself as I shove the painting under my bed.

I go back downstairs where Cassie is lying on her stomach on the floor, nose to nose with tiny Princess. What a good distraction. We go up to my room with the largest mugs of tea I can make and sit down on my bed. I perch the tea on the sill and fish out my biggest sketchbook. I can sense the painting beneath the bed like a beating heart.

It's decided: I'll take care of the scenery, and Cassie will take care of the people. I picture the high street of the town where I've lived all my life, a street I've been looking at and walking down for eighteen years. I start sketching on the thick, heavy paper. This is a vision of the Weston Bay I actually know, not some outdated idea of what it once was, as if the past is some kind of guarantee of quality. Cassie points out things to add, little elements of the town that

I've forgotten, shop fronts that would stand out. We go back and forth, each thinking of a place, a detail – the old-fashioned sweet shop Daisy and I were allowed to go to once a week when we were little. The blue-haired elderly lady who walks three huge Doberman dogs (almost as big as her) up and down the high street every day. The bus driver who looks like a wizard with his long grey beard and rings on all his fingers.

'We're working on something,' I say, when Mum pops her head in to enquire about dinner.

'You still need to eat, though,' she claims. Which I suppose is true. 'And you can't starve Cassie either. You can have it in here, I don't mind. I'll make you a bacon and egg sandwich, shall I?'

'Alright, if that's OK with you.' She disappears. I'm so lucky to have a mum who doesn't push me or press me or ask me too many questions. She'll just let me and Cassie do our thing in peace and provide the sandwiches. I wish things hadn't played out the way they did with Señor Mango Sorbet. I wish it wasn't just going to be Mum and Princess in a few weeks' time, I wish she had, you know, a real person to hang out with. I wish I hadn't had to get involved. But I would do anything to protect my mum, the way she's done with Daisy and me for all these years.

Once we feel satisfied with the look and feel of the high

street, Cassie takes over and blocks in the people on the street. The real people who live here. People who look like her as much as people who look like me, women who wear headscarves, men who hold hands with men. We transfer the sketch to A3 paper, but this time instead of soft grey pencils, we use pen and ink, creating the same image except more neatly, and in bold, graphic strokes and bright, eye-catching colours. It looks like an old advert from the 1950s for weekend trips to the coast, except the time is now. The people are now. This is our town and the 'our' grows and changes with every passing year. We leave space for a banner at the top and the final task is for Cassie to meticulously hand-letter 'NO PLACE FOR HATE IN WESTON BAY'. All fired up and working away, she looks more beautiful than ever, twitching her nose in concentration and holding her breath like it's the difference between getting something perfect or messing it up.

Finally, we stand back and look at the work we've created together.

'It's perfect,' Cassie says.

'Yeah . . . it is.'

'There's just one problem, though.' She turns to me, looking concerned.

'Which is?'

'There's only one of them.' She's right. If we're going to

be any match for the hate campaign, we'll need more than one poster.

'It would be mad to do all of them by hand, wouldn't it?'

Cassie looks at her watch, chunky and digital and bright purple and just extremely Cassie. 'It's taken us three hours to do one. So yes, it would be mad to do all of them by hand.'

'And it's too late to go to a copy shop today,' I say.

'And we don't know if someone in a copy shop would be on board with our project . . .' Cassie says, reminding me of all the things I can't even *see* because of my privilege.

'No, totally, you're right,' I say, ashamed. 'We just need to find someone trustworthy with a large format printer-copier thing. Surely there must be someone. Between the two of us.' I bite my lip and try to think hard, going through my mental Rolodex of people I know even a little bit. This is what happens when you, essentially, have one friend.

My phone vibrates and I see it's Cal ringing me. I feel my heart rate start to increase but it's not because of romantic flutterings anymore. I'm nervous at the thought of having to figure out how to act in front of Cassie, what tone of voice to use, how affectionate to be, and what my goal is. I guess I'm trying to figure out what my . . . game is.

'Huh, it's Cal,' I say, staring at the phone in puzzlement.

'Oh,' says Cassie, looking a little anxious, like he's about to spoil all our fun.

'Hey . . .?' I say, finally answering the phone.

'Hey! Are you alright? You sound . . . weird.'

'I'm fine, just hanging out with Cassie.'

'Plot twist!'

'Yeah, I guess that was kind of predictable, huh,' I say, smiling at Cassie who's sitting on my bed. We're a good team.

'I had a break in my shift and thought I'd ring to say hi, see what you were up to. I just had to clean up a kid's puke. It was bright blue from the slushy he'd just consumed, which was, naturally, the origin point of the puke itself.'

'Eurgh, gross . . . you have my deepest sympathies.'

'So now I'm hiding out in the back office, hoping no one disturbs me until the end of my legally mandated break.'

'Your office . . .' I say, and if this were a cartoon then my eyes would have widened incredulously. I see Cassie raising her eyebrows at me, stretching out her hand in a 'go on!' gesture.

'Yeah?' Cal says, understandably perplexed by why I would want to know about the behind-the-scenes administrative workings of my local cinema.

'Say I'd made something that needed copying a few times

. . . but it was quite big, like A3 –'

'We have a colour copier in here, you know? It can print and copy large format – we need it for the rotas and stuff like that,' Cal says, enthusiastically.

'And you'd let me use it?'

'Sure. What's it for, though?' He finally sounds a little suspicious.

I sigh. 'You know those horrible posters around town?'

'I assume you're not about to tell me they're your doing?' Cal jokes.

'Hilarious! But no. Cassie and I have spent the evening making something to replace them with.'

'You don't have to ask me twice to help out on a noble cause. To be honest, I would have said yes to something half as good. My shift finishes in like two hours? Do you want to meet me here with your stuff?'

'Amazing – you're the best,' I say. 'See you in a bit.'

'I'm glad I called you!' Cal says. A little stab of guilt prods at my stomach. 'I didn't expect to end up with a side quest tonight. See you later.'

When Cal's shift ends, we're loitering in the foyer, our masterwork transported to the cinema in my old A-level art portfolio.

'Hey,' he says, kissing me on the cheek. 'Hey, Cassie.'

'Thank you so much for this!' Cassie replies. 'We really appreciate it.'

'Yeah, we do,' I say, and hug him tightly. He looks a little bewildered. But I want him to know that I think he's great.

'It's no problem. You can't come back there, obviously, because my manager is prowling about, but if you let me know how many copies you want, I'll bash them out for you,' he says with a warm smile.

'Ten?' Cassie asks, anxiously.

'I'll do twenty, why not.' Cal shrugs. 'It's not my photocopier!' He elegantly swipes the portfolio from Cassie's outstretched hand. 'Want some help putting them up? I assume you're doing it under the cover of darkness.'

'We would love some help, but we thought about that, and Friday night in Weston Bay is not the time to be sneaking about doing potential vandalism if you don't want to get detected. We were going to regroup later in the week when it's a bit quieter,' I tell him.

'Maybe Wednesday night?' Cassie suggests. 'You know . . . to take our minds off results day?'

# CHAPTER FOURTEEN

'Hey, cutie pie!' Cassie calls to me as she steps off the bus. I envy her, that she can be so easily affectionate. There were so many moments during our shift today where I felt so awkward just being near her. Urgh.

I smile back. 'Hey!'

'How's it going?' she asks as she drapes her arm over my shoulder and we start walking towards the centre of town. Has she got more touchy-feely recently or am I just hyper aware of it? Maybe this is her way of overcompensating for the tension that's been bubbling away.

'You mean since I saw you like four hours ago?' I ask.

'Yeah!' She takes the roll of posters from me and rests them on her other shoulder, gallantly.

'Weirdly . . . not much. Daisy actually asked me how work was today, though!'

'That's progress, right?'

'Yeah . . . I feel bad. I feel like we're cutting it pretty fine to sort stuff out. I literally can't believe this stupid fight has hung around for so long.' Results day is TOMORROW which means uni isn't far behind. I don't want to be without my sister for much longer – things are too *polite* and *careful*. I need to fix it.

'You two will sort it out – there's no way this is going to last forever. It just won't,' Cassie says, giving my shoulder a reassuring squeeze.

'God I hope not,' I say, wondering if maybe it's time for me to swallow my pride and talk to Daisy properly.

We walk in silence for a few seconds. 'Cool that Cal's going to help us. Always useful to have a charming white man to deflect any suspicion. And to take the heat, if necessary,' says Cassie.

'I really hope it's not necessary!'

'Same, especially since we're very obviously doing a good deed here.'

'But yeah, it's good of him. I haven't actually seen him in a while, you know . . .' I say, realizing as I speak how much I've been avoiding seeing him in person. I feel horrible. I spend a lot of my time feeling horrible at the moment for one reason or another. At least the anxiety around everything else seems to be fighting for attention over my anxiety around results day.

'No?' Cassie looks at me, surprised. I shake my head. She doesn't ask anything more.

When the time comes to do our work, it's quiet, as we

predicted. The three of us roam around, trying to remember all the places the fascist posters had been, and taping ours up in their place. It's only a small gesture, but it feels good to be turning something we're naturally good at – making things – into one little way to resist the tide of hate in this town. To say this is our town too, and you don't get to define it on your terms.

I keep thinking about how incredible it felt to make the posters. Just to create something. And, more than that, to create something *useful*. It's such an amazing feeling. And tomorrow I find out whether I'm headed for three years of history and theory of creation rather than just creating things myself. But I can't focus on that. I need to focus on this. A potential parting gift for my home from me and Cassie.

After we've trudged all the way around town, we're finally out of posters. We collapse on the steps of the war memorial, Cassie and Cal sitting on either side of me. I keep sneaking glances at Cassie, like a compulsion. Cal reaches for my hand.

'We make a good team,' I say, smiling at Cassie. Sneaking around after dark for purposes other than going out . . . that's a new thing for the day.

'I'm proud of us.' She smiles back, a devastating, radiant smile. I look at her and don't know what to say. I'm looking at her a moment too long, the silence hanging awkwardly between us.

'*You two* make a good team, I'm just along for the ride,' says Cal, mercifully shattering the silence. I wonder if he knows how right he is.

We all leap to our feet and begin our journeys home. I hug Cassie tight when her bus arrives, and she even pulls Cal in for a hug.

'Right,' Cassie says, fixing me with a stern look from the door to the bus. 'Tomorrow. College. We got this.'

I swallow down my nausea. 'Yep.' I nod. 'We got this.' The doors close behind her and with that she's gone. The next time I see her, it'll be the moment of truth. The moment the future gets set in stone.

Cal and I walk on, hand in hand, my guilt coagulating in my chest, Cal mercifully ignoring my damp palm. 'I was thinking,' says Cal, just as we're reaching the point where we need to go our separate ways, 'maybe I could stick around a bit longer. I know I was planning on going home properly at the end of September, but all that can wait. We could see where things go, with us I mean.'

I feel hot all of a sudden. 'Oh! Right . . .'

'I haven't done anything about it yet,' he says quickly, maybe sensing my surprise. 'It's just something I was thinking about. No pressure, obviously.'

'No, no, it's not that I don't want you to stay,' I say. 'I just hadn't thought about it. But it's not up to me. It's your life, it's your decision.'

'Yeah, of course,' he says, looking down at the pavement, tracing a circle with the toe of his trainer. I feel so grateful to him for all the help he's given me with this covert operation. How he let me use his office equipment when he could have got into big trouble. How he's come out in the middle of the night to stick the posters up with me. How he's always just so *there* and so good and so kind and so cute. I'm not at all surprised that my sister fancied him. But I don't think I can let this whole thing roll on indefinitely. I can't keep lying to him and to myself. Besides, Leeds is looming at the end of the summer. So if Cal doesn't leave Weston Bay, he'll be another person I need to wrench myself from if and when I do.

He gives me a kiss and leaves. I feel exhausted when I finally make it home. Physically and emotionally. I can barely believe that I have to go through results day tomorrow on top of it all.

And things are still weird with me and Daisy. It's felt like a weight around my neck for days and days and days. I just want to make things right. Results day I can't control. Me and Daisy, though? Maybe I can control that. I miss her. I miss our in-jokes and our kitchen dancing and how she gets so excited about soil and how well she knows me.

I knock on her bedroom door, interrupting the quiet in her serene little nest.

'Daisy,' I whisper loudly after lurking on the landing too long. 'Are you awake?' Too late to chicken out now.

'Well, I am now, you idiot.' A good way to begin.

'Sorry,' I say, inching around the door and into her room. She flicks on the lamp next to her bed and sits up, disgruntled.

'What do you want? Why aren't you in bed? It's results day tomorrow.' She rakes her fingers through her long hair and fixes me with a hard stare.

'I wanted to talk to you.'

'Huh,' she says, cocking her head.

'I'm just so tired of how things are between us. I'm sorry. I just wanted to tell you that. I'm sorry.'

'What are you sorry for?' Daisy asks.

I breathe in deeply. 'I'm not sorry about Cal. I just want to start by saying that.'

Daisy plays with the ends of her hair, twisting them around her finger. 'This isn't a great apology.'

I sit on the end of her bed and take her hand, the way I used to when we were little and I was scared of being in the playground without her. 'But what I *am* sorry for is changing the plan without telling you. Daisy, we've been together our whole lives. Nursery, reception, primary school, secondary school,' I say, counting them off on my fingers. 'It was always me and you together. Always me and you getting lumped together as if we were just the same person. And then when we had to be separated for sixth form, I thought, OK, this isn't so bad. Maybe I kind of like a little separation. Some time apart. So I know we talked about going to the same uni and being back together again, but when it came to it, I thought, you know, maybe it would be better if we just kept on down this path. I don't think I understood it was so important to you. I don't think I even really understand it now.'

'Do you want to understand it?'

I nod sincerely.

'You went to sixth form and you met Cassie.'

I squint at her in confusion. 'But you have loads of friends – why does it make a difference to you that I met my best friend?'

'Because you stopped talking to me! It was like you just didn't need me anymore. I was always your, you know, Default Person, and then all of a sudden I wasn't and it made me realize how superficial all my friendships were. Not like they're superficial people, but it just wasn't anything close to the bond I had with you. I could have fun with them but it wasn't the same. It made me realize how important you were to me. I'd taken it for granted my whole life because we're sisters, and you think that bond doesn't need any maintenance, and it made me understand that it does. I thought we would get it back at uni, that we would regain that closeness that we had before. And then you just decided to do your own thing.'

'Daisy . . . changing the plan is the biggest mistake I've ever made.'

She looks up at me. 'Serious?'

'I literally don't sleep sometimes, thinking about how much I wish I wasn't going to uni. I feel like I'm losing my mind. I'm so anxious about leaving here, and you, and Mum, and Cassie. Just leaving everything. Leaving my life. It feels like everyone around me is so *hyped* to start this new chapter in their lives and I'm just not ready. Maybe being with you would have made a bit of a difference, but I don't think it would have solved it. I'm just not ready to leave it all behind. It makes me feel like an idiot baby.'

'You're not!' She squeezes my hand. 'It's your life and you know what's best for you. You don't have to do it if you don't want to.'

'It's too late for that now, I think,' I say, breathing in sharply and twitching my nose. I realize that's Daisy's symbol of disapproval and it makes me smile a little through the hurt. 'And I guess tomorrow I'll know for sure whether I have to leave or not. But honestly, I had no idea you wanted us to stay together. I thought I was the one who couldn't deal with the world while you were sailing through life.'

She shakes her head. 'No way.'

'So why were you always telling me to have friends other than Cassie?'

'Because I knew how it would feel for you when that's gone. Ahd I didn't want that to happen to you.'

I flop sideways onto her bed. 'I'm sorry I made that decision without talking to you. I thought it was only me that it hurt. I didn't know it would affect you, too. '

Daisy seems to be thinking carefully about everything. She strokes my hair and pauses for a moment. 'I'm sorry about the whole Cal thing. I was a bitch.'

'Ha!' I say, grateful for a laugh. 'You were a bit.'

'You deserve someone brilliant. I was just jealous. I guess you were right when you said I wasn't used to you getting something I wanted. I feel like such a shit sister.'

'While you're already feeling shit . . .' I venture.

'What?'

'There's another reason why I felt like we should be a bit more separate . . . you say some things that I'm not really comfortable with. You make these little comments . . .'

'Like what?' Daisy looks confused.

'Um . . .' I say, trying to figure out where to start. 'Well, you'll talk about how you don't want to get fat or about how skinny you're looking, or you'll make tiny digs about how I look or how inactive I am. I mean, you don't always actually say it like that, but . . . it's what you mean, right?'

Daisy's face has reddened. 'No . . . not like that . . .'

'But that's what it sounds like to me, you know? It makes it difficult to be around you sometimes because I feel like I'm being judged all the time, and I don't feel that way when I'm with Cassie.'

'Shit,' she says, looking at the carpet. 'I really don't think of you like that . . .'

'Like what?'

'Like . . . you know, fat?'

'But I am! And that's OK, you know? It's really an OK thing to be. I'm happy with my body and with who I am. So, I guess I just wanted to tell you, that when you say things like that it reminds me that you think it's not an OK thing to be. And that makes it harder for us to have a relationship, you know?'

'I hadn't thought of it like that . . .'

'I have to think about it all the time,' I say, forcing myself to smile so she'll know that I'm not still angry about it. 'It would be nice not to have to.'

'I don't know where those thoughts come from sometimes . . . they just pop in my head, like I can't help it? Like talking about the weather, just normal. But I know it shouldn't be normal. I know that.' She looks at me, earnestly. 'I'm going to work on it, I promise.' Daisy says, looking down at her hands, inelegantly digging some soil out from under her thumbnail with one of the many bobby pins strewn around her room.

'Good,' I say. 'It can be your new thing for the day.'

Daisy looks up. 'Huh?'

'Oh . . . yeah!' I realize 'I've been deliberately trying to do one new thing every day this summer. Like . . . to prepare myself for going away. Cassie's been helping me come up with something weird every day that I've never done before so that by the time I leave, I'll be more adventurous and ready for . . .'

'A world of new things,' Daisy says, gently.

'Yeah.'

'I love you. And I hope you don't get the grades to go to Leeds,' she says, smiling.

I laugh. 'I love you, too. I hope you get the grades to go to Bristol and you change the world.'

She beams at me and pulls me into a hug. I'm so relieved

that things with Daisy are better, I nearly cry. 'Do you want to stay here?' she asks.

'Yeah,' I say. And that night, squashed up in her single bed, we sleep fitfully, both dreading the morning.

# CHAPTER FIFTEEN

Today's the day. I don't even get a choice in what today's new thing will be. A-level results have been thrust upon me by the universe.

Cassie's parents have reshuffled some staff around so we can have today and tomorrow off, and even though I don't have to wake up to go to work, I'm awake even earlier than I would normally be. Daisy's sleeping next to me, and I stare at the ceiling in her bedroom, thinking how perverse it is that I'm anxious about *getting* the grades I need to go to uni, rather than not getting them.

I know Daisy's been up half the night, I could tell by her breathing, worried that she won't get the grades to do her physics degree. You know, like a normal person. Not like me, feeling backed into a corner and heading towards a future I hadn't really thought through. It's not like I didn't choose this. That's the problem here. I'm the architect of all of this, and now I want some hand to descend from the heavens and rearrange all the pieces on the weird chessboard of my life. And my best chance of that is if I just don't get the grades to do my course. Or even the grades to get into my insurance choice, which is also miles away. At least today is the end of it. Today's the day when I need to accept that the future is really happening, and maybe when I get confirmation, it won't be as bad as I think it will be? The existential dread pressing on my chest seems to think otherwise.

College at 9, yeah?

Cassie. She's decided to do an art foundation course, work, keep making art and see what she wants to do the next time UCAS applications open. A novel approach and one I should probably have considered myself, rather than feeling pressured into going down the academic route because my sister and I are meant to be clever. I send Cassie back a GIF that's appropriately terror-filled, and once it feels like a reasonable time to get up, I nudge Daisy.

'You awake?' I ask.

'What do you think?'

'I think yes.'

'You think correct.'

'Let's have breakfast then head out?' I ask. 'You can accompany me as far as the bus stop on your walk.' We're going to two different places – me to college and her to our old school where she stayed on for sixth form.

'Urgh, I don't know if I can manage breakfast . . .' she groans.

'But it's the special-occasion special!' I protest.

She sighs. 'I guess.'

In our pyjamas, we head downstairs where our mum is plating up smoked salmon and scrambled eggs. The elusive special-occasion special. Usually only seen on birthdays and Christmas, but clearly A-level results day has been designated an important enough event in the calendar of Lily and Daisy Rose to warrant it.

'I was just about to wake you up!'

'As if we were asleep,' says Daisy, rolling her eyes and plonking herself down in her usual seat at the table.

'I'm just glad to see you two have got over whatever was bothering you for the last couple of weeks,' Mum says, turning to the table with our breakfasts. 'I came to check on you last night to make sure you were okay and you were sleeping in the same bed like when you were kids – it's too much! But honestly, Daisy, I don't know what you think you have to worry about – I saw how hard you worked all throughout your A levels. You're going to do just fine. You too, Lily.'

'That's what I'm worried about,' I mumble. We eat our breakfasts in relative quiet except for the insistent mewling of Princess who's been temporarily shut in the living room because the smell of the smoked salmon is making her so crazy. Very cute but very annoying. Then we head upstairs to get dressed for the Big Day.

'I'm so sorry I can't come with you . . .' Mum's standing at the doorway, biting her lip regretfully.

'You literally have a job to do, Mum,' I say.

'The animals of Weston Bay won't thank you if you skip work to come get our results with us,' says Daisy. 'Think of all the little cats and dogs and hamsters and snakes. And we'll text you straight away, won't we?'

'Yeah,' I say, waving goodbye and heading up the path with Daisy. We walk together as far as the bus stop, where I pull her into a tight hug. 'You've got this in the bag. You're the best person in the whole world, and Bristol would be stupid not to take you.'

We pull apart and she smiles at me. 'Well, I mean, that's one hundred per cent true. And with my awesomeness, I'll pray that you don't get the grades to go to Leeds. But even if you do, we'll figure it out.'

I have to remind myself to breathe on the bus because it feels like an elephant is sitting on my chest, and it's only when I get off that I realize I've been grinding my teeth the whole time.

Cassie is waiting for me outside college in a purple

sundress and a bleached denim jacket. Her brown legs are so well-moisturized they almost look like they're glowing. I feel weird for looking at them now, as if I haven't seen them hundreds of times before. I try to shake off the guilt – I have enough to deal with today.

'Have you been in already?' I ask.

'No way! I'm waiting for you!'

'That's very nice of you, I don't know if I could resist my curiosity that long.'

We turn to face the building and she resolutely holds out a hand. I look down at it, wondering if she wants me to shake it. But then I realize she wants me to hold it and I pause for a moment, but finally I do, my palm slick with sweat not only about my results but about the fact that this feels like flying too close to the sun somehow. It doesn't seem right to hold her hand with everything that's going on inside my head. Can she feel my feelings through my skin?

We walk into college and head towards the long trestle table where large brown envelopes are laid out in alphabetical order by surname. As Palmer and Rose, Cassie and I are heading for the same end of the table, sidestepping classmates who we would ordinarily stop to chat to, but who are today in a world of their own.

'Godspeed,' says Cassie, dropping my hand and reaching

out for the envelope with her name on it.

I pick up mine, turn it over in my hands. It feels like a lead weight. I just have to accept my fate. I decided it all, anyway. I made all these choices, whether or not I think it's fair that we're expected to make the exact right choice when we're seventeen. It was still my choice. And whatever is on the inside of this envelope, I'll have to come to terms with it.

I swallow hard, breathe deeply, and open it, sliding out the white sheet of A4 paper with my subjects and grades printed at the top. The spiky peaks of the As jump out at me. This is it. This is it. It's all really happening. I'm really leaving. I'm really going to university. I'm really going hundreds of miles away. Even though I knew this was coming, I'm completely unprepared for this moment and wildly ill-equipped for what's just around the corner. But as I stand there, dry-mouthed, in the corridor at college, I wonder for the first time if it's actually a good thing. If leaving for another city means that I don't have to deal with my feelings for Cassie. It could be the perfect time for a fresh start. A clean break. But it would also mean not seeing Cassie and I'm not sure that's an option for me anymore.

I thought that by now I would have tried so many new things that the familiar things wouldn't seem so important, but . . . but . . . even though I've had loads of fun, I can't help feeling like it was all a distraction from the real problem. Nothing important has changed. I don't want to go. I just don't.

I feel a hand on my shoulder. 'So?!' Cassie asks, excitedly, gripping her own envelope.

'Yeah, I did it.' I smile weakly. 'How about you?'

'Somehow I managed to do, like, *really* well?!'

'Maybe that's because you're a genius?' I suggest. We're interrupted by a couple of former teachers who have come in to congratulate, commiserate and guide the ones who need the commiserations through the UCAS Clearing process. But I'm not really listening to anything. I'm in my own little bubble. Self-preservation. Trying not to engage with anything or anyone because I don't know what I want to say. I remember to text Daisy to find out how she did, even though I know she's smashed it. I remember to text my mum to tell her that I got the grades to go to university.

As we're trudging down the long corridor, Cassie grabs me by the arm. 'This is where I first saw you! With your bleeding ankles!'

I smile at her, glad for her sentimental streak. It makes me feel a little bit safer in how much I love her. 'It feels like a long time ago, doesn't it?'

'Feels like yesterday.'

'Don't you think you've changed since then?'

'Not really,' she says. 'Why, do you?'

I bite my lip. I wonder if I've changed or if everything I feel now was in me all along. Did I know when I applied to universities that I didn't really want to go? That I just felt like I should apply because that's what everyone else was doing? Was I always bi? Or is that something that was only ever going to reveal itself to me by knowing Cassie? I can never know. All I can do is sit with all of this knowledge and try to make better decisions in the future. 'I don't know.'

Finally, we walk out of the building for the last time.

'So . . . what do we do now?' Cassie asks.

'Yeah . . . I hadn't really thought that far ahead.'

'I feel like we should . . . drink? Something?'

'Yeah, I guess so . . .' I say. I really do want a drink. Or four.

'But also it's, like . . .' She looks at her phone. 'Quarter past nine. Shall we just go back to mine and watch films until it's an appropriate drinking hour?'

'Yeah, that sounds good,' I say. I'm relieved to see a text pop up on my screen from Daisy which is just a line of party-popper emojis. Not a huge surprise, but reassuring none the less. Great success in the Rose household. The soon-to-be-empty Rose household.

We walk to Cassie's house half a mile away towards the centre of town. Every so often Cassie leaps in the air and clicks her heels together like she's in a musical.

'I thought your grades didn't matter?' I ask.

Cassie frowns at me. 'Just because I'm not going to uni this year doesn't mean they don't matter to me. I mean, I want to do well, but also . . . I am going to go eventually. I think. I don't know. It's nice to have options, right? And my parents will be *delighted*.' I'm lagging behind a bit and she looks over her shoulder at me.

'Yeah . . . I guess.'

We arrive at Cassie's house via the corner shop where we buy a variety of delights, before installing ourselves in front of the TV and scrolling until we find a channel that plays back-to-back episodes of Kardashian-flavoured shows.

'I'm *obsessed* with Scott's career in property development! This is how you celebrate,' Cassie says, before tipping crisp scraps into her open mouth, as on the TV they contemplate another multimillion-dollar purchase.

'Truly, this is the life,' I say. I'm joking, obviously, but there aren't many places I would rather be. It's a place to hide from real life. And a place where I get to be with Cassie. It's hard to look at her now. It almost breaks my heart. I sneak glances at her when we're watching TV, out of the corner of my eye.

'What?!' Cassie catches me.

'Nothing!' I say, insistently. Cassie smiles slyly but doesn't say anything. 'Oh! I'd better text Cal . . .' I see he's already texted me to ask me how it's all gone, which is annoying even though it's nice, because I wanted to get there first for once in my life. Cal is another person who makes me feel guilty. I wish things could've stayed uncomplicated with me and him. I wish I could have kept feeling the way I felt towards him at the beginning. But whatever I felt for Cal was always mixed up with my issues with Daisy, and now it's all mixed up with how I feel about Cassie. I got into something with him because I wanted him, and I liked feeling wanted. I needed to know what it felt like to have something that other people wanted – that my sister wanted. I stayed in it because he's so kind and thoughtful. He made me feel so sure of myself. But those are all the reasons why he deserves something better than what he's got with me. He doesn't deserve to be stuck in a relationship with me, now I know that I love Cassie, not him. I should have broken up with him a week ago, I know it. But he feels like a soft blanket, comforting and warm and a safe place to be while I'm so uncertain about what's actually going on with me.

*No*, I remind myself, *I need to break up with him. I need to tell him not to stay in Weston Bay just for me.*

That's amazing! Btw I just walked past someone taking a photo with one of your posters!

'Cassie!' I look up from my phone. 'Cal says he just saw someone posing with one of our posters! How wild is that?!'

'On the one hand extremely wild, on the other, they are perfect works of art, so not surprising at all.'

'It was an honour and a privilege to work on it with you,' I say. She beams and then wriggles along the sofa and rests her head on my shoulder, her hair tickling my neck. I breathe in the smell of coconut oil and the warm scent of her body. I sit very still, as if she's a bird that'll fly away if I move too suddenly. My arm feels dead and achy but I don't want to lose this moment. And then I feel like I hate myself again. The guilt is back. That feeling like I'm doing something wrong by feeling like this around her without her knowing won't leave my brain. I'm a mess.

Sometimes I let myself think about how the conversation would go: how I would bring it up if I could. How it would play out. And all I can ever see it ending with is hurt and confusion. She'll think about all the time we've spent together and how I was looking at her through a different lens. The fact that I'd been fancying her all this time would colour all of her memories of the time we'd spent together. She'll say that we were never really on the same page at all and then she'll never speak to me again. I can't put us through that. It's not worth it, just to get it off my chest. All for my own benefit. I can't lose my best friend.

It comes as a relief when Cassie leaps up to go to the bathroom and I reposition myself on the sofa. When she returns and sits back down, my body is facing away from her.

Halfway through the fifth episode, Cassie and I simultaneously get texts from Ines in our A-level art class, telling us that everyone's going to the Crown tonight and then taking the bus to the one shitty club in Seaforth. I'm surprised she thought of me, but it makes sense for Cassie to have been invited. She was always a bit more outgoing than me. I guess Ines knew we came as a pair. For now, anyway.

'Shall we?' Cassie asks.

'Yeah, why not.' I shrug. I'll finally get to have a drink and take some pressure off for a few hours. I'm trying not to think too much about the big Going Away situation. I just want to take a day off from the whole thing. 'Except,' I say, biting my lip regretfully, 'I look a bit of a mess, don't I?'

'I mean, I don't think so,' says Cassie with a shrug, 'but there's no reason why I can't loan you something from the Cassie Palmer archives . . .' She hoists herself off the sofa and disappears upstairs.

I'm about to call after her to remind her that we're

simply not the same size, but then she's back, holding an oversized cocoon dress in a paisley printed cotton. 'Try it on!' Cassie urges. 'This one's actually made from fabric from, like, a roll, rather than a recycled pillowcase. That's how you know you're special.'

I go out in the hall and try it on, delighted when it fits. It's beautiful: short and flirty and I feel kind of hot in it. The magic of Cassie Palmer. I return, twirling as I enter the living room, and Cassie gasps. 'My god, I'm a genius.'

Our plan for the evening set, we nip back to the corner shop for some booze and drink a couple of cans while Cassie does my eye make-up. I try not to think about how close she is to my face or how warm she is. I definitely do not think about what would happen if I cupped her face in my hands and brought her lips to mine. Damn – I'm out of beer.

We agree on one more drink so we can finish watching the run of episodes we've become weirdly invested in while only half paying attention. Even now, Cassie's on her phone, flicking between watching Insta stories with the sound off and scrolling through her main feed. Suddenly she yelps, 'Oh my god, look at this!' and holds the phone up to my face. 'It's our poster!'

She's right. It is our poster. Under the railway bridge, photographed in broad daylight by Taylor, a pretty, gentle boy with long blond hair, who hardly ever spoke in our politics class but ended up always saying the most interesting things when he did feel emboldened to contribute. The only caption is a yellow emoji fist of solidarity.

'It feels funny knowing they're out there and people are seeing them, right?' I ask, smiling.

'Yeah! I'm so hyped that people are responding to them!' Cassie's beaming. 'I know, in the grand scheme of things, it wasn't much. But it was something.'

When we get to the Crown that evening, a large group of people from college are already congregated around a booth. Many are halfway through a drink already.

'You came!' Ines says, extending her arms to us. She's all big eyes and charmingly gappy front teeth and seems genuinely pleased to see us. 'I didn't think you would!'

'Why's that?' I ask.

'You two hardly ever came anywhere! Highly party-avoidant.'

'We came to parties sometimes!' Cassie says, refusing to accept Ines's assessment.

'Sure,' Ines says. '*Sometimes.*'

'Anyway, we're here now,' I say with a shrug. 'Cassie, do you want a drink?' But she's already been pulled into a conversation with Taylor. I wonder if she's telling him we were behind the posters. I walk up to the bar and order a glass of wine for myself and a pint for Cassie. I set it down in front of her but accept she's temporarily lost to me. I feel pathetically untethered. I stand around for a moment, sipping my wine, when Ines reappears at my side.

'So, what are you up to next year?' she asks. 'I can't remember.'

'I'm, uh . . .' I swallow hard. It still feels strange to say it, especially now it's actual reality. 'I'm going to do art history at Leeds.'

'That's amazing!' Ines says. 'That'll be so interesting, you'll love it. You always were more knowledgeable about the background and the theory. The rest of us were just good at making things.' It feels nice to hear her say that. To know that I stood out to her in some way.

'Thanks for this,' Cassie says, grabbing my wrist to attract my attention and holding up the pint in the other hand. She turns back to Taylor. I guess we *have* been hanging out all day so I can't feel too rejected. What did I expect, that she would just stay with me all night long and I wouldn't have to talk to anyone except her? I really need to be less pathetic if I'm going to survive in the real world. Which I now know is completely unavoidable. I down my wine in rapid gulps and go to the bar to buy another. Naomi from my AS-level history class appears next to me and I let her pull me into her group of friends without worrying too much what she thinks of me or if I'm saying something stupid.

I drink some more and then some more and before I know it we're on the bus to Seaforth. I can barely keep my eyes open but it's OK because I'm sitting next to Cassie and I want so badly to put my arms around her and lean my head on her shoulder and just fall asleep there. I want to tell her how I feel about her, then disappear so I don't have to deal with any of the fallout. I don't want to stick around for the confusion or the mistrust. I just want to press pause on everything and not have to keep moving relentlessly into the future and away from everything I know and love.

I barely know what I'm talking about with Cassie, but before long we're all piling off the bus into the warm evening air, cut through with a cooling sea breeze. The group of us, probably about eight or nine now, but I feel too drunk to count, head to the Vault: the dark and dingy club in Seaforth which is open late-late rather than just late. It turns out that everyone else from college had the same idea as us and I pinball between people I vaguely know, drinking a mysterious blue cocktail which is suspiciously cheap.

I'm trying to force my drunk mind not to think about Cassie at all. But I find that what I think I'm doing and what I'm actually doing aren't exactly the same. Drunk minds have a way of doing what they want. I have short but enthusiastic conversations with what feels like a vast array of people who I didn't really speak to at college, but tonight the alcoholic haze and shared emotional academic trauma makes them seem like the best people in the world. Ines's boyfriend Harry has some kind of surprisingly rich family, which we find out because he produces a flash-looking debit card with a flourish and proceeds to buy us a tray of shots.

Through it all, I am hyperaware of where Cassie is in the room. It's like she's the only source of light and my flickering gaze follows her like a moth to a flame. She's giggling loosely with Taylor on the edge of the dance floor, her back leaning against a high table. What are they talking about? What is she feeling? I can't live like this. Someone, maybe Zahra from my English class, pulls me onto the dance floor and we drunkenly sway to the music as I down yet another drink, drowning my fears and feelings. I can't remember the last time I drank this much – I don't know if I've ever drunk this much. But it's the night for it, right?

Cassie throws her head back, laughs, and touches Taylor's shoulder.

I just want to forget and suppress and forget and suppress.

But what if I didn't.

What if I just let myself shake off all my inhibitions? What if I just went for it? Would it really be so bad? Maybe it's the shots talking but . . . maybe I should just do it. I start to move towards Cassie then stop in my tracks.

It's very clear that any minute now, Cassie and Taylor are going to start making out. There's a fist grabbing at my insides. This is just going to be how it goes, I guess. I'd better get used to it. What am I expecting, that she never goes out with anyone for the rest of her life? What right do I have to feel any of this?

I'm going out of my mind on the dance floor in this dingy club. I turn away, grab another drink and dance and dance around our group until I'm suddenly possessed with the need to talk to Cassie. I can't stay away from her.

She's still deep in conversation with Taylor when I reach out and touch her shoulder. They haven't kissed.

'Finally!' Cassie says emphatically, her head rolling slightly. At least it's not just me that's feeling messy. Within seconds, Taylor has already wandered off. 'I thought I wasn't going to get to dance with you!'

We dance together, giggling delightedly at the goodness of the pop – 'How Will I Know' by Whitney Houston – the very best. I feel softer already, melting into the moment. Maybe things aren't so bad. Maybe I can live with the fact I struggle to look my own best friend in the face, the fact that I don't want to go to university, let alone one so far away, and the fact that I've essentially been leading on lovely Cal all summer. Maybe I can live with it all.

Cassie grabs me by the hand and lazily spins me around. I kind of lose my balance and she reaches out a hand to steady me but instead I fall forward into her and she puts her arms around me and holds me tight. She presses her cheek against mine and I feel her breathing.

'I love you, Lily,' she says.

'I love you, too,' I say, a little awkwardly. The lights overhead are flashing blue and moving fast.

'No, I really love you . . .' Cassie says insistently, like it's a competition. As if I don't mean it enough. I tilt my head back to look at her and she's so beautiful even under these flashing blue disco lights, and now I've let myself feel that raw, real love for her big brown eyes and her heavy, black eyebrows and her soft, brown skin and her big thighs and her huge smile and her perfect lips—

And all of a sudden I kiss her. It happens. It really happens. My arms are around her waist and I can feel that strip of soft skin in the cut out on her purple sundress and her hands are in my hair and I can smell her face cream up close. Everything's all familiar but I'm seeing it in a new light, from a new angle, so much closer, and it's the best, scariest feeling I've ever felt.

We're kissing right here in the middle of the dance floor and we don't stop for what feels like an eternity and a split second at the same time, but when we eventually pull apart she looks at me with something like horror, runs up the stairs and out of the club.

*SHIT.*

# CHAPTER SIXTEEN

When I wake up on Friday morning it's actually Friday afternoon. I have no memory of how I got back in my bed, but I'm glad I managed it. My head is pounding and my mouth is dry and—

Oh god.

I just remembered.

I'm going to throw up.

Oh god. This is the very, very worst.

I ruined everything.

That look keeps replaying over and over and over. The raw betrayal in her eyes . . .

How could I do it? Why would I do it? Is vodka really that powerful?

In the cold light of day, *of course* it's obviously a huge mistake. Of course I wouldn't dream of telling Cassie in a million years that I'm in love with her. What possessed me last night?!

All I had to do was hold on a few more weeks until I was miles away and we would never have had to deal with it at all. But I just couldn't, could I? I had to indulge some stupid, destructive impulse and now here I am, all self-loathing and hungover at the end of the world.

I'm going to be sick.

I roll over and feel around on the floor for my possessions. Yep, all still there. And my phone is even plugged in to charge, which is something that I definitely wouldn't have done in whatever state I was in last night. I fight the urge to vomit down the side of my bed and roll back into the foetal position, now clutching my phone and squinting at the screen. I can't believe it's not broken.

There are no messages from Cassie at all.

But there is one from Cal.

Call me when you wake up.

Urgh. Poor Cal. I can't believe I let it go on this long and get this far.

I don't call Cal. Instead I lie in bed and look at the ceiling, wishing myself to sleep again so I can ride out this hangover. Or you know, I could just go back in time and not be such a dickhead. I really, really need to see Cassie today. I need to clear the air and explain myself and see if maybe, just maybe, we can get to the part where we can just move on. I'm completely mortified. While I'm laying there, I hear a gentle tap at the door.

'Lily?' Daisy whispers loudly.

'Come in,' I croak. She pushes the door open.

'Yikes.'

'Yikes indeed,' I say, patting the bed next to me for her to come and sit down.

'I can't believe I finally got to meet my crush . . . and in such dramatic circumstances!' I have no idea what she got up to last night, but Daisy clearly isn't as hungover as I am.

'What do you mean? Which crush?' I'm looking at her out of one eye, in the hope that if I keep the other one closed the room won't spin as much.

'Your actual boyfriend?'

'Cal? Where did you meet him?'

'Jesus . . .' Lily laughs. 'Don't you remember?'

'No . . .' Oh god, now what? What fresh hell?

'He brought you back here last night when you were too drunk to like . . . do anything. He said you called him rambling and crying in a drunken mess. He went and picked you up and propped you up on the bus and made sure you didn't vomit or get hit by a car or anything.' Now I really want to cry.

'God. This isn't really like me, is it?'

'No, not really,' says Daisy. 'I thought we were having a

pretty wild time at Katie Lewis's party but you really went there.'

'I honestly want to die. Please, Daisy, kill me. It would be an act of love. An act of mercy,' I say, reaching up to put my hand on her shoulder.

'It's just a hangover, you'll live.'

'But I don't want to,' I wail.

'No choice. You've got to. I need you,' Daisy says, at which point I hear another knock at the door. I'd forgotten Mum would be here. It's her day off.

'So you're alive!' she says, brandishing a bottle of Lucozade and joining us on the already cramped bed. It reminds me of when we were little and me and Daisy would leap into bed with Mum at the slightest opportunity, just to be close to her. That thought makes me want to cry too.

'I was just saying to Daisy that I would quite like to opt out of that.'

'It *is* just a hangover, and I don't want to be "that mum" but *please* don't do that again, especially not when you're off at university and there's no nice boy to pick you up and bring you home safely,' she says. She puts a hand on my head. And I burst into tears.

'Oh my god, what's wrong?!' Daisy looks pale and horrified.

'It's not so bad! It's only a hangover! I just don't want

anything to happen to you!' Mum exclaims.

'It's all such a mess,' I say through loud sniffles. The floodgates are open. It's all coming out now. Including me. 'I don't want to go to university! I just felt like it was something I had to do because Daisy was doing it and it would make you proud of me. I just want to stay here and keep painting and figure out what to do next. I don't want to leave next month, I really don't,' I ramble semi-coherently. 'And I did something really bad last night and I've messed everything up and I just don't want to leave the house ever again or see anyone or do anything. I want to hide forever.'

'But . . . you're you,' says Daisy. 'You couldn't have done anything that bad!'

'I really did, ugh, I hate myself, I hate everything.'

'Just tell us,' Mum urges. 'It's what we're here for.'

I sigh, my whole body shuddering. I'm not used to having to tell people things. I never usually have anything to tell. 'I . . . kissed Cassie. Which is obviously terrible because she's my best friend *and* because of Cal. I feel like the worst person, I can't believe I did it.'

Mum and Daisy nod thoughtfully.

'We'll come back to the Cal thing in a moment,' says Mum. 'But I just want to check, so we're on the same page, that the problem isn't so much that you kissed Cassie – but the problem, as you see it, is that . . . you meant it?'

I nod silently. I hate that this is such an unfamiliar thing for me. I hate that I feel so vulnerable, telling people how I'm feeling, being honest with myself. I hate that *telling the truth and asking for help* could be a new thing. But it is.

'OK,' says Mum. 'I get it, I get why that feels like a big thing.'

'And you're upset because you're worried about hurting your friendship with her,' Daisy continues.

'Yeah,' I sniffle.

'That figures,' she says, before adding quickly, 'I mean, not that I think you're right, but I just get where you're coming from. That's a natural problem to anticipate.'

'I guess I just felt sort of . . . filtered towards boys, like that was just how it was going to go. I never really thought too much about it, because obviously I *do* like boys. But I guess I like girls too. And then Cal came along and obviously he's such a catch,' I say, finally no longer crying.

'Ha!' Daisy says, smiling.

'I know, I know . . .' I muster a smile too. 'And I guess it felt nice to be wanted in that way, you know? I've always felt kind of . . . behind. But I think maybe that was just because I was sort of fumbling around, not really sure what I was looking for.' What I don't need to say, because I know Daisy understands, is that it felt nice to be wanted in that way by someone Daisy wanted. But what good is it to be wanted by someone that you don't want? Where does that actually get you?

'And you know that now,' says Mum.

'Yeah. Is that OK . . . with you, I mean?' For a horrible moment I'm sure she'll object. 'You don't think I'm stupid and attention-seeking?' I think back to my breakfast with Molly, the scathing way she talked about Georgia from school, how I fear people would perceive me the same way.

'I don't think, for one second of my life, that I've ever thought you're stupid. And yes . . . whatever you want to do, whoever you want to be with, that's OK with me.' She sounds bemused to even be asked, but just hearing her say those words feels like sunshine. 'Uncle Michael will be delighted!'

'Thank you for not saying that you knew all along. That means a lot,' I say. 'I felt like everyone was always deciding things about me and it made it hard for me to make my own mind up about what I wanted. And I guess about, like, who I am.'

'Only you know. It doesn't matter how long it took to get there. You're eighteen years old, you're still a baby.'

We sit in silence for a moment, me lying on my bed, Mum sitting up by my head and Daisy down by my feet. I'm not sure if my bed can actually take the weight of three people but I don't want to ruin the moment by mentioning it. And besides, it won't be my bed much longer, anyway.

I bravely sit up even though it makes the room spin. 'Can we start trying to solve some problems?'

'We can!' Daisy says.

'All is not lost. These are fixable problems, and if not necessarily fixable, then containable. Deal-withable,' Mum reassures me.

'OK. First and most urgently: Cal,' Daisy says.

'Obviously I do have to break up with him, don't I? I can't just sort of . . . not.' I know I have to. There's no escaping it.

'I'm definitely not saying this so that I can ask him out.' Daisy grabs my arm comfortingly. 'Which of course I won't. But . . . yeah. You do have to, I think.'

Mum narrows her eyes at us. 'This isn't what you two were fighting about, was it?'

Daisy and I look at each other shiftily.

'Bloody hell.' Mum shakes her head. 'I thought I raised you two smarter than to fight over a boy!'

'Sorry, Mum,' we mumble, dutifully.

'If it makes you feel any better, he wasn't really what we were fighting about. He just opened the floodgates to some other stuff we needed to work out,' Daisy says.

'Well, that I can deal with. Listen, I'm not saying that Cal should be your boyfriend but I do want to state for the record that you must definitely keep him as a friend – not only did he go to the trouble of bringing you all the way back here in one piece, he also stayed to have a cup of tea with me once you'd been put to bed,' says Mum.

'God, it just gets worse. Why is he so *nice?*' I yell. 'I hate that I've messed him around like this. I just hate it.'

'He's by no means the worst person you could have accidentally fallen into a relationship with,' Daisy says.

'I know,' I say, picking at a flake of paint on the windowsill. 'Me and Cassie met him and his friend on the same night and I guess I just thought if she was going to pair off with some guy I might as well too. I just didn't know he'd be so . . . good. And, like . . . he really is good. He's so sweet and hot and calm and, yeah, I do really fancy him. Just not enough. Not as much as . . .' I trail off. Even thinking about her makes me feel sick, the way I torpedoed our whole friendship in ten seconds last night.

'Well, hey, that's one problem partially solved. You know what to do about Cal.' Daisy shrugs, as if it's the most obvious and straightforward thing in the world to break up with someone.

'And then there's . . . the future,' I say.

'This isn't a new thing, is it?' Mum asks.

'No.' I shake my head. 'I've been worrying about it for months. I just don't want to go. Or maybe I just don't want to go now. I don't feel ready at all. I don't feel sure of what I want to do. I want to keep making art, I want to have the time and space to do that, to get better at it, to learn and figure out how I want to use it.' I pause for a second. 'You know those posters around town – the ones that replaced the white nationalist ones?' I ask.

'Yeah?' Mum and Daisy say in sync.

'That was me and Cassie.'

Daisy beams.

'Wow! You two make such a good team,' says Mum.

'We'll come back to that,' interrupts Daisy, clearly wanting to stay on track with the various issues that are presenting themselves right now.

'But yeah . . . I just feel like I want to do more and I don't want to give it up to study something academic. It doesn't make sense for me. Just being kind of clever doesn't feel like a good enough reason to do this. But it's what's happening. I've let it all go too far.'

'You're not on death row, Lily,' says Mum, and even though she's rolling her eyes and sounds exasperated, there's something comforting about it, like maybe it isn't all as serious as I feared. 'It's not like there's no way out of this. You know that, right?'

'Not . . . really?' I say.

'I'm never going to force you to do something that

you're not happy with. I could tell you that maybe you'll get to Leeds and you'll love it and you'll feel right at home straight away and love studying. But you know best what's right for you. It's not too late to change your mind.' Mum frowns at me like she really wants me to understand what she's saying.

'I . . . don't have to go?' I ask incredulously.

'No . . . it was your idea, remember? I didn't force you into it! And besides, it's not like the university is going to disappear if you change your mind and want to go in a year or two's time. I don't want you taking out student loans for something you're not serious about!'

I laugh. I properly laugh. I feel like a huge weight has been lifted instantly, to the extent to which I almost can't believe it. I can't believe I have the option to change my mind. I feel like the luckiest person in the world.

'Yeah, don't you remember, this all started because you saw me filling in my UCAS form and said you might as well if I was?' Daisy says. She's not wrong. I just can't believe that was all it took for me to end up feeling so consumed and overwhelmed with anxiety for such a long time.

'God, I'm such an idiot,' I say.

'No, you're not,' says Mum, reaching over and stroking my hair. 'Why don't you tell them you've changed your mind and you're not coming, I bet loads of people are hoping to get in through Clearing. They'll probably be grateful to you for dropping out!'

'Is it dropping out if I never even showed up?'

'Probably not,' she says pensively. 'If you really don't know what you want to do, why don't you do the art foundation course at the university in Lansdowne. It's not like it's that far away on the bus. It'd keep you busy. Keep you practising. Then you can see how you feel in a year's time, maybe go to university then, or maybe not?'

'You're a genius,' I croak out. I take a sip of the Lucozade and silently thank the universe for my brilliant mum.

'Which leaves one remaining problem to solve,' says Daisy, not willing to let us lose momentum on our stampede through my fears and anxieties.

'Yeah . . . the big one,' I say.

'It's funny, you would have thought that detonating your imminent plans to move city and start a degree would be the big one,' says Daisy.

'Unfortunately not,' I moan.

'You can't avoid Cassie forever,' says Mum. 'She's your best friend.'

'She's kind of your only friend,' says Daisy.

'Yeah, I'm going to work on that, I swear,' I say.

Daisy yawns and stretches. 'I'm relieved to hear it.'

I sigh dramatically. 'I just don't know what to say to her.'

'What do you want to say to her?' Mum asks, reaching across to the cord of the blind and pulling it up. I guess I can't live in a dark little hangover cave forever.

'Nothing, I just want this all to go away.'

'But it won't just go away,' Mum says soothingly. 'None of this stuff has fixed itself by you ignoring it, has it?'

'No. I guess not,' I mumble, taking another sip.

'So,' says Daisy. 'What do you want to say to her?'

I think for a second. 'I want to say that I'm sorry for kissing her so unexpectedly and for crossing the line and that I'm sorry for messing up our friendship and making her run away from me last night.'

'But you don't want to say that it was a mistake?' Mum asks.

'It was a mistake to do it. But it wasn't a mistake to feel it.' I close my eyes and again feel the rush, the rightness of the kiss, the sense of it. And then the shock and the pain of the look of disgust on her face. She didn't look back as she left the club.

Mum sighs. 'It's a tough one. I feel like you should tell her the truth. Do you think you'll be able to hide it for the rest of your friendship if you write it off as a drunken accident now?'

'I'll be able to do *anything* if she only forgives me and still wants to be my friend.'

273

'How did she react?' Daisy asks.

'She sort of went with it at first like it was drunken fun, but as soon as we pulled apart, she ran.'

Daisy pouts sympathetically. 'I'm sorry. It *is* a tough one.'

'Mum's wise,' I say, pawing at her hand.

'I'm not that wise, I accidentally had several dates with a married man.'

'OK, but like . . . except for that,' Daisy says, reassuringly.

'Then my wisdom on this specific issue is that you shouldn't avoid Cassie. You should tell her the truth and see if that dynamic is something she can deal with, you know? It doesn't have to mean the end of the world for you two.'

I know she's right. I know that's what I have to do. There's no getting around it. I can't hide in here with my Lucozade and my potential sick bucket forever. I have to face the world at some point. I have to talk to Cassie.

'Right, so what's the plan?' says Daisy.

'I need to break up with this great guy, drop out of uni before I've even turned up and tell my best friend I'm in love with her,' I say, smiling drily. 'No big deal.'

Mum looks at me with such love that I think I'm going to cry. 'You're stronger than you think you are,' she says.

'First deal with uni, then deal with Cal and then deal

with Cassie,' says Daisy. No time for crying. Only time for getting things done.

'Alright . . . I think this Lucozade might have magic powers, I actually feel capable of standing upright now. No wonder I didn't feel ready to leave my family.'

'The culmination of your Summer of New Things: deal with your shit!' Mum says with a wink.

'Just checking you understand that I'm still going to Bristol,' Daisy says, looking at me seriously. 'I'm not going to stick around here just to hang out with you, you know.'

I laugh. 'Yes, I understand that. I hope I'm allowed to visit you sometimes.'

'Promise.'

'OK,' says Mum, looking over her shoulder as they head out of the room. 'We'll leave you to it.'

Dealing with university is surprisingly swift and painless. If only all my business today could be quite so seamless. I mean it was an administrative nightmare just to get through to the university helpline, but once I'm talking to a human instead of the weird robotic answer machine, it's fairly straightforward. I almost want to drag it out because I *really* don't want to get to the next item on my to-do list. I take my time getting dressed to try to put it off but it's no good.

It's time to deal with Cal. Toes curling in my trainers,

horrible, spiky butterflies fluttering around my stomach, I do as he asked and call him. At first I think he's ignoring me but he picks up on the last ring and answers in a low voice.

'Hello?'

'Hey . . . it's me.'

'I know it's you, your name comes up on the screen,' he says. I can't tell by his tone exactly what he's thinking.

'Right . . . I just wanted to say—' I start, but he cuts me off.

'Just a minute, I'm meant to be checking in the screens for people filming or whatever but I'm just going to sneak out the back for a second, hold on.' I can hear him walking and breathing. A door opening and slamming behind him. 'OK, I'm back.'

'I just wanted to say thank you for making sure I got home last night.'

'You were a total mess when you called me from that terrible club in Seaforth – like, unbelievably drunk! There was no way I was going to just leave you there.'

'No, it was honestly so, so kind of you.'

'Obviously I didn't know you were going to dump me on the bus back to Weston Bay . . .'

Oh. Now this . . . I was not expecting. 'I did that?'

'Yeah . . . obviously it bruised my ego a bit but . . . this doesn't really work, does it?'

'I really wanted it to!' I protest. 'You're, like, the greatest guy in the whole world. You're so fit it's almost unreal. *And* you're really nice. To everyone. You made me feel wanted and . . . and . . . *wantable*. I didn't know that was possible before I met you! It felt really special being with you.'

'Ha, thanks,' he says. 'But it's OK. I really like you – all this doesn't change that, you know? Or at least, for me, it doesn't have to. You're cool. And you'll always have a place to crash if you're in Auckland.'

'God,' I say, nearly crying. 'I thought you were going to, like, berate me?'

'Jesus, no! Like I said, you were a mess – you were crying about how much you were in love with Cassie and how I was too good for you and I just couldn't let you get home on your own. I thought you were going to get hit by a car or something.'

'That's so embarrassing, I can't believe I said that to you,' I say, feeling hot all over. 'I can't believe what a mess I was.'

'Neither could your mum! Who's great by the way. She said this was most out of character for you.'

'It really is . . .' I mumble.

'Look, Lily, no harm done. I liked you a lot. You're super pretty and really chill to spend time with, but you need to do what's right for you.'

'Oh Cal . . .' I say. 'Please can you come over soon, for dinner with my mum and my sister and me? I think it would be really nice.'

'Sure, why not,' he says, genially. 'Unless you're trying to set me up with your sister. You did mention that last night!'

'Jesus, what *didn't* I mention?'

'Not much, to be honest. Look, I think I'm gonna get rumbled any minute for using my phone on my shift so I'm gonna go now, but I just wanted to check you were still alive and not feeling too deathly.'

'You're the best.'

'I guess I am,' he says. 'Bye, Lily.'

'Bye, Cal,' I say back. 'But . . . you haven't seen the last of me.'

'I hope not, you know,' he says, and before I hang up, it's like I can hear his smile through the phone.

I sit on the side of my bed for a minute, marvelling at how dramatically everything has changed for me in twenty-four hours. How much I needed Mum and Daisy's help to figure it all out, to feel supported enough to change my life. But I'm still left with one big problem.

Cassie.

I take a deep breath and look down at my phone again. My hands shaking, I find her number in my contacts and press 'call'. As soon as I do it, I want to throw up. I listen to it ring, praying that she won't answer. It rings and rings and then as soon as I hear the ringing stop I immediately hang up. A phone call was a mistake.

I text her and ask, as casually as humanly possible, if she wants to meet up tomorrow. I leave my phone in my room and slowly make my way downstairs to watch TV with Mum in the living room. I know if I take it with me I'll just be checking it every ten seconds, as if the fact she hasn't already texted me today isn't bad enough. Daisy joins us after watering the plants in the garden and Princess is mewling adorably on my lap. After numerous episodes of a food programme involving increasingly absurd eating challenges, we all eat together. I manage to swallow down some ravioli with butter and sage and drink about three pints of water to rehydrate. With every breath and every mouthful and every heartbeat I think about Cassie and will her to have texted me back.

When I go back up to my room and pick up my phone, I already know she hasn't replied. There's nothing. With the heaviest heart I've ever felt, I text her one more time and tell her that I'll be on the bench at the end of the pier at eleven o'clock tomorrow morning, and if she wants to see me, she knows where to find me.

# CHAPTER SEVENTEEN

I'm trying to sneak out without being noticed. Trying to dash to the pier to meet Cassie. I'm honestly too nervous to have a coherent conversation with anyone. But Daisy hears my footsteps on the stairs and darts out of her room.

'Is it now?'

'It's now,' I say grimly, looking back up at her.

'You're taking the painting, right?' Daisy asks, emphatically.

'What painting?' I have no idea what she's talking about.

'The one you did of Cassie, duh,' she says, holding her hands in front of her in a gesture of pure frustration.

'Why would I take that?'

'Come on, Lily,' she says, holding a hand out to me and dragging me into my room. 'I thought artists were meant to be romantics. What better way to show your love for someone?!' She folds her arms and stands in the door, keeping guard until I've rummaged under my bed for the canvas and she's seen me, with her own two eyes, put it in my tote bag.

'Now,' she says, seeing me off at the front door. 'Go get your girl.'

It comes sooner than I could have ever anticipated. 10:55 a.m. It's creeping dangerously close to the appointed time. And I still haven't had any reply from Cassie. But I'm here, where I said I would be. It's a beautiful day: the sun's shining from behind fluffy clouds and there's a light breeze bringing a sweet sense of relief from the heat. When I first got here, I wondered if it was a good omen that the bench was free, or a bad sign that Cassie wasn't already sitting on it. I haven't been able to come to a decision on that yet.

My heart is pounding so hard I'm surprised I can't see my chest vibrating. I have no idea what I'm going to say to her if she does show up. Hard as I tried, I couldn't formulate any kind of excuse about results day that made sense to me or that said what I wanted to say without ensuring instant rejection and embarrassment.

I check my phone to see what time it is, which once again shows me Cassie hasn't been in touch. It's eleven o'clock and there's no Cassie-like figure stomping down the pier. I feel a lump rise in my throat. Although I knew it was possible she wouldn't show, I hadn't actually thought through how it would feel when she didn't. The stinging heat, the panic of being so alone, the lost friendship which I might never be able to repair. It feels like I'm watching her run away from me in the club all over again. I close my eyes and steady my breath. I listen to the sound of the seagulls. The sound of the sea. I feel exhausted. I wish I was at home with Mum and Daisy and Princess, safe in our little cottage. But I'm here. And it's eleven fifteen.

I hadn't decided how long to wait for her. But fifteen minutes feels like more than enough for someone who's never late. I close my eyes again and start counting down from ten. If she isn't here by the time I open my eyes, I have to go. I can't let myself sit here all day, hoping she'll show. I have to accept it.

10…

9…

8…

7…

6…

5…

4…

3…

2…

'Lily! Oh my god, thank god you're still here!'

And there she is. There she is! *Cassie*.

Flustered and sweating and pale, but there. No purple lipstick. No gold lamé. Just an oversized black T-shirt and leggings. She's still the most perfect person I've ever seen. 'It's been such a nightmare – my phone is broken, I dropped it the other night when I was pissed – the keyboard is just completely fucked, I can't reply to anything and my bus was stuck in a traffic jam and I couldn't even unlock it to call you let alone text you! I can't believe how much I rely on it, it's embarrassing.'

'You're here,' I say in disbelief. In those ten seconds all I could see was Cassie's horrified face when we kissed, all I could think about was how there's no way she'd want to see me again knowing how I felt about her, and that she was probably making out with Taylor at that very second rather than coming to talk things over with me.

'Of course I'm here,' Cassie says. 'I was so relieved when you texted me.'

'Relieved?' I ask.

'I was so . . . embarrassed? And mixed up, I guess. And I was just grateful you even wanted to see me.'

'But why?'

'After what I did? Kissing you like that.' She shakes her head and closes her eyes. 'Ugh . . . it was just . . . so stupid of me?'

I feel confused and honestly a little thankful that she thinks she instigated it. I guess maybe I can get away with writing it off as just a drunken accident. But that wouldn't